ALICIA FREILICH

OLD GREEN LADY

Translation by Brigitte Weitzman

eRIGINAL
Books

Published by Eriginal Books
Miami, Florida

www.eriginalbooks.com
www.eriginalbooks.net

First Edition: Comala, 2000

Second Edition: Editorial Eclepsidra, 2015

ISBN: 978-1-61370-092-1

PROLOGUE

Patience: Alicia Freilich's exuberant prose

"The reader will remain taken aback at images that flow with great power and which make memory point to various historical moments and characters from the Venezuela of yesteryear"

The novel Old Green Lady by Alicia Freilich (Caracas, 1939) is a text in which a prose of great exuberance unfolds. Indeed, thorough rich textures, the author builds several discursive levels that point to what was the change of the political system and the collapse or "mudslide" which meant the Bolivarian revolution that replaced the democratic system that prevailed in Venezuela until 1998.

This multiplicity of levels and musicality of speech become a sort of kaleidoscopic events where the experiences of Fulgencia are in the foreground; a mature woman who suddenly, and with a life somehow "made" is experiencing a country where all the known values and references have been disrupted in pursuit of an alleged sea of happiness that never came and, at this point, although the official discourse holds otherwise, it will never come. That fact of having to start from scratch after the raze that meant the arrival of a political caste that demolished everything is just what the title of the piece refers to, to the need of being resilient in this new reality. The assembly of the narrative levels recalls the typical jazz and Latin music forms. There is, if one wants, a sublime representation of what the tempo and the creole urban rhythmic is.

The referents relating to the popular culture also abound in the story. The reader will remain taken aback at images that flow with great power and which make memory point to various historical moments and characters from the Venezuela of yesteryear. It was masterful the reference to the Vargas mudslide of 1999, in the sense that the event itself is the artificer of the artifact. All the anecdotes that begin appearing after around the protagonist are related to the collapse in all orders that meant the arrival of Chavez. Additionally, the communication phenomenon that meant the revolution, as well as the media reading that said information machinery gave to each one of the characters, as well as to historical events, it is well stated in the text. To this it refers precisely the way how in the second part of the novel the protagonist appears pursued by various security bodies, all had among them contradictions regarding the character after which track they were. I think the nuances that appear in these sequences, beyond the aesthetics of the detective novel, have very kitsch hues, in the style of the "secret agent" of the sixties.

It is important to say that any gradation of an erotic nature that may appear in the text is rather secondary; the point here is a deep reflection about the political and social future development of the nation.

Perhaps the lengthy experience and expertise of Alicia Freilich as an observer and writer of a country that has undergone profound changes through its various historical periods give her a superlative perspective about the identity and ultimate implications of the Venezuelan. This author has had a substantial contribution to the nation through her years writing texts of great keenness for El Nacional, as well as for other major media. Also, her contribution through the audiovisual media was extremely relevant.

Freilich ultimately extends an invitation to the Venezuelan of today to reflect in relation to the present reality; its causes and who are we, as well as the path to which the national future is headed. I think that beyond the aesthetic considerations around this powerful prose, there is in the background a work that responds to a sensible questioning, and a proposal to the reader for the opening of a new territory where there prevail freedom and values of the individual, beyond the abstractions of a group that has served as a pretext for the systematic violation of individual rights.

We attend with this novel by Alicia Freilich a very settled work and where everything responds to a profound elaboration; this text is a tribute to an author who has had a persistent and decisive contribution to the work of our cultural values and our historical consciousness.

JOSE ANTONIO PARRA
El Nacional Literary Paper - March 28, 2016

THE DISTORTED GLOW OF A SOCIETY

The novelist writes in his novels the lives that he has failed to live, used to say the novelist of the Jews in distress Bernard Malamud. But for that, the novelist has to recreate sometimes the society in which he would have liked his characters to live. Or himself. And since the mirrors usually store the light with the diligence with which the old people treasure memories, this of the mirrors often is the artifice that the writer uses determined to put before the eyes of his readers the result of the recreated society. What happens when it is the delicate function of putting characters in sight, the novelist decides to do so in a concave mirror? Well, there happens what can be noticed in the admirable novel just published by Alicia Freilich with the title of Dirty Old Lady (edicionescomala.com). The author of *Old Green Lady* uses a character full of symbolism that began his path a long time ago in Comic strips. This is the ineffable Don Fulgencio. And what if Don Fulgencio were a woman? And what if Dona Fulgencia would have acted in a society like the Venezuelan over the last half century?

To begin with, Dona Fulgencia who misses her opportunity to study, for not submitting to the discipline of a career to finishing it, at least with a nursing, pharmacy technician or haute couture seamstress diploma, becomes on the basis of her religious beliefs in Bibles saleswoman. "Offering myths, processing prophecies, financing miracles, managing grief and remorse, it is a sublime and daring enterprise that can deliver good dividends of ecstasy. With that in mind she decides to start her new profession for the Buena Estrella lottery stand in her beloved San Jose, and at the door there is a sign that warns: "cash today, credit tomorrow yes". - How can I help you, Missus? -Good day. I offer bounded bibles of all types and price -Bibles, you say? —You can buy them in easy installments - And what religion are these bibles from? If you read this one, for example, you have read them all because any of them is not the doctrine of a sect but history of religion.- How is that stuff?- You didn't understand? Not a scrap- don't speak oddly to me? How is it possible that you don't understand me mother?-You are not down to earth, my daughter, that is why I want you to study a practical career —You are tormenting me, I don't like Biology, numbers or business- It is a matter of trying, insisting- I am not interested- You should learn a trade, a skill in something concrete so that you can stand up by yourself. You know that when I was a young girl I took a course in basic accounting which has helped me to manage the store, if not, where would we be today? You father is a merchant of chimeras, a person in continuous levitation."

Inclined for what her father was rather than by the mother's advices, young Fulgencia will follow the path of the fatherly chimeras.

But beyond the craft of selling bibles, Fulgi has to go populating her life as any human being of stories that help her to understand the world in which she happens to perform. The substance that nourishes the argument with which that this precarious biography is tacked in time are the lyrics- time-appropriate lyrics. Let us not forget that the author of the novel will offer us a concave vision of a world that is the Venezuelan of the past fifty years. And under this, for example, it is not that the lone man is the one who releases his loves in an inflatable rubber doll; it is the lone woman who chooses a male inflatable doll for exercising seduction.

Fulgencia's encounter with the figure the night of love is an insuperably constructed novel. And this under the sofa of the song: The woman who does steal glance at love does not deserve to be called a woman ... The woman has a magical language that must be learned with kisses ... according to what Alfredo Sadel sang, so consistent in meaning to Fulgencia as Marx's *The Capital* for a revolutionary.

Already Vazquez Montalban, before being an author of, airport literature masterfully described, with the support from songs, the passage of an eventful era as was that of the Franco dictatorship in Spain in *Spain's Sentimental Chronicle*.

Forty years later, the author of *Old Green Lady* has attempted it with equal success, in the Venezuela that has become what it is. Because the history of Venezuelan society of this past half century underlies as an epiphenomenon in the lyrics of the songs that provided to those of us who have lived in this society a value of references and quotes to support the validity of our existence in this society.

"Missus Fulgencia, excuse me, we asked you for a front photograph card size, and of course yours, is this baby your daughter or your granddaughter? Oh, forgive me, with the rush I gave you my own photo that I always carry with my documents. When I get this oblivion attacks, I look at it and remember whom I am, where I go, so I don't lose my way, do you understand?" That's what sums up the fact that the author knows so well, not only the songs each era in which Dona Fulgencia has to unfold, victim, at the end, of the mudslide occurred in 99 in Vargas , and a politically persecuted person for her subversive adventures in which the fate irreverently masquerades of irony .

And it is not only the songs from each era in the past Venezuela, it is the deep knowledge of jazz that the author, here and there, boast about. A music director, not so famous or so ignored, said that jazz will be the classical music of the next century. Alicia Freilich, author of *Old Green Lady* has drawn from her nook this classicism to which, one day, will be reduced the Venezuelan life, and the one which the most attentive historians will not be able to tell us about the vicissitudes of everyday life at that time.

In this effort to turn around things, Freilich's novel has not omitted capturing that poetic aroma that adorns every life however trivial as it happens with Dona Fulgencia's. Discovering the poetry that contains the trivial, Borges was inimitable. But it is not in the Argentinean writer on whom Alicia Freilich bases in the poetic reference, but in two poets, one of the Venezuelan eloquence and the other from the Brazilian, Eugenio Montejo and Eugenio de Andrade. There is a place ... where you lived and in the dream, sometimes you still live ... And the words of Montejo: My vertical century and full of theories... I cross Marx Street, Freud Street ... I walk around a bank of this century with its wars, its post-wars and its Hitler drum far away between blood and abysses...

Verses as frames that serve as a vehicle to this novel, the same way as the taste and color disguise the real effectiveness of certain drugs.

Alicia Freilich has written a period book, an important social document to review the life of Venezuelan society, with dialogues in which there calm down the words that in each of the seasons has used the Venezuelan as coordinates of expression and all within a literary structure which indicates that *Green Old Lady* is a leading edge novel that will enter into the Venezuelan literature through the noble door of history door. If Stendhal claimed that a novel is nothing else but a mirror on the way, Old Green Lady reflects the reality of the Venezuelan long way in the distorted sheet of a concave mirror. The concision with which it has been written, verging on savings, belies the saying, by another way, that in literature saving be the basis of misery

ATANASIO ALEGRE
El Nacional Literary Paper -January 2002.

The questions of my granddaughter Adriana enlightened this idea.

SHE ALONE IN SIXTY YEARS

1

THESE ARE TIMES OF REVOLUTION. Merely six months, but the terms of the agreement must be changed before signing and knocking down together. It is time to get ready the best one can, pleasantly and calmly. Being punctual is perhaps the most revealing sign of seriousness before the one who grants such bail for life... – Where are the keys? At the bottom of the sea, Matarile-rile-ron...

The day seems warm and cloudless. Early she searched for it through the crack. The shack, which has neither a laundry sink or a washing machine, it does have a sole window facing north, no panoramic view and gives her only a piece that offers a glimpse of the rest. But every day she needs it more complete. Large and of pure velvet. It is, forever, her beloved hill Avila. Some want it to be Waraira Repano, but it depends on each person.

Put make up on?... *Mariamoñitos invited me to eat plantains with rice.* But, there are just three blocks to the meeting place. Besides, they know each other so well. How to fool the one that sways and arouses her, touches with wisdom every pore, intuits from afar her smell and patiently runs through her creases. No. She goes as she is, as she has been, as she came and as she shall depart this world. Do not be distracted, hurry up... *Let's go to the citronella orchard, to see Doñana cutting the parsley....*

They still call Avenue of the Samanes the bare treeless street where she begins her journey. Almost no trace to assume that this area was once the countryside and much less flowery. Miraculously, still some bush dares to tilt its dry branches on an old portal. The towers are born, grow, develop and do not die, on the contrary, they are proof of reincarnation. She has to leave soon the rented room in the old ailing building where she lives -stone oasis in a glass desert -because it shall be resurrected. Small bricks with enamel, colored glass and the guard house, shall give it the facial charm that the season requires.

At full speed, with the vigor of a new martial era, she walks on the sidewalk that if you look well, it retains a surprise that has just begun. The gray lines of the Hopscotch carved into the pavement. As she goes by, the choir of soloists expands from the balconies and booths – There goes the crackpot – She does not look as a loose woman, poor soul, she looks rather prudish – Do not believe it, there are stories about her that are disgusting and give you goose bumps. – Neither a beggar nor a marginal person, each day more eccentric and mysterious this neighbor.

Her sneakers, a blue-jean almost transparent due to many hand washes with a cheap detergent, her matted hair in a ponytail, the duffel bag, her body as lean as the splinter that her footsteps break, nothing weighs, not even her somewhat bulky belly, and she can then move the pebble as she did over there in San Jose, playing Hopscotch with just one foot inside the boxes painted from one through ten, a pretext after getting out of school, for running into, without fear or guilt, the heartthrob in her San Jose del Avila Parish... *Rice pudding, I want to get married, with you yes, with you no... I know how to sew; I know how to embroider and to set the table in its holy place...*

Feeling free, is it a natural or acquired right? Who knows. But it is a luxury paid with the high cost of the abyss between two solitudes, the desired one and the imposed one. Reliable company shall be what she is looking for renewing the agreement that shall be signed within half an hour. She is sick of the ideas and turns in the childish game Tealight – I want your kiss – Over there – I'm looking for a job – Over there – Give me your hand so I don't fall – Over there – I am counting on your friendship – Over there – And while playing it, she allowed them to steal the most precious and irretrievable thing. Time.

She stops because at the corner of the second segment the traffic light is red. One does the same thing in Las Cuarenta Matas, one learns the art of passing bending down, or running, or staying still as a post. It depends. The goal is to beat the mouse and the cat, asking for "time out", and this way you reach your bunker alive. Now, if you have to speed up, oh, oh. Your tasty torment awaits.

When the light turns green, she stealthily approaches the rusty fence that the employees left open. Oh oh, she can then snoop comfortably inside the event planning agency which occupies the whole block and nurtures the capital city having fun with the revolution.

Imagine the circus celebration, real stylish clown costumes, tables and plastic chairs, the magic top hat, piles of chocolate and cookies, a DVD that amplifies the noise, the latest rockets, and the Barbie made of cardboard, inflated, to be broken using a stick, in a net row, awaiting the turn. *Sawdust, the timbers of San Juan, they ask for cheese, they ask for bread, the Rique ones for candy, the Roque ones for cheesecake...* Her piñata was a Mickey Mouse filled with goodies and confetti, in the main patio of the house, decorated for such a great occasion, and reprimands do not lack- Kiddo, take advantage of this free scramble – My sweetie- do not waste the bargain and throw yourself with the others to collect even scraps –You have to stand in the line of children to receive your piece of cake – If you become sadder, you are looking for the way to be separated from everything in the maid's room.

It is getting very late to remember but in exchange for these live comedians, there were puppets of the Ugly Duckling avenging itself, Pinocchio lying, Tarzan and Cheetah, while gobbling up a *bienmesabe* cake, meringues, and tisane. Have fun! How will the new sweets be?

The wait is almost over, what thirst, how she longs for him, but she must take advantage of the emptiness of this great space for parties, the place is perfect to play Hide and Seek, you run and run, the boys should not catch the girls, or you rather be in the center of the circle as the Blind man's bluff, turn and turn blindfolded, or leave your jewels pawned until you fulfill the punishment, do twenty laps around the playground, swallow a spoonful of salt, insult the doorkeeper, and this way they return the ring.

Jeez, in a large classroom as this luxurious warehouse they set up the theater and the contests of the school year. There she became an expert in pretending triumphs – Today you shall be a maiden lost in the forest and appears the prince again on a horse – Is your turn to tap dance and make faces. Now you take the role of a peasant in love who marries the master.

And all with the happy ending. While waiting during the rehearsals she was a leader marking 0 and X playing Tic-Tac-Toe until achieving a line spanning three equal and continuous signs. The award is to get out arrogant, sharing the mockery about dumb nagging

adults. *The girls were laughing at this poor Don Ra-*
mon, because his shoes had no heel and no toe ...

Very sweaty and taking in Pig Latin: *onderful-way-*
ime-tay: she leaves the room that announces a future
full of parties, daily shows, yeah!

She passes by the door of two villas now modern
place for the dead, where she is offered a funeral
cocktail preceding the burial. She looks at it out of the
corner of her eye. Right there they had a wake for
Juan, Carlos, Aristides and Oscar, such opposites in
life, so evenly matched in the horizontal rite of the
casket, and condolences, such pieces already of their
wonderful whole.

The house and the burial day before, was a kingdom
of freedom while the old people were praying. We
would play Hide and Seek. Hiding in terror and joy is
the clandestine. Under, above and behind the strange
furniture, discovering rooms and corrals of others,
challenge the ghost and shoo the skull... You will
never find me!...

Just a bit more, palpitation drowns and to relieve the
desire a sweet is medicine. Just outside the mansion
of the dead, a kiosk and a cafeteria grant soberness.
Coconut macaroons, marshmallows, and guava pre-
serves in the small shop. Bonbons, profiteroles, stru-
del, Oreo and Choc-Ice on the glass shelves... *With a*
real and a half I bought a monkey, the monkey had a

23

little monkey, I have the money, I have the little money, and I always have my real and a half... In the pause to resume the road where he awaits for me, there comes an ice-cream seller on wheels. How tasty, how yummy, licking the ice-cream in the left hand, skewering the perinola with the right hand. In the backpack there is the aluminum miniature doll, a gray spin top and the Sunday comics' supplement.

What can be read now if Charlie Brown's gang lost the dad, and even Mafalda, this precocious little old lady sleeps a long nap? Anyway, nobody has as much fun as The Little King, Donald Duck and Bambi. There are no more oceans for Sinbad, giants for Gulliver, princess for Cinderella and Snow White, no wonder countries to tell about. There is just the wolf disguised as a refined military, tender grandmother, but his lie does not stand a line. It can be already seen what he is trying to hide while the people are distracted with the vast empire of space odysseys, galaxies in war sounds corny... *Once upon a time there was a little boat, it could not sail and if this story, and if this story seems short we shall tell it again... One, two, three, four weeks went by and it could not sail... Rains, storms and hurricanes came and it could not sail...*

Damn! How slow, you will miss the alliance, run, do not be foolish, enough of childishness, you are too old

for that, you are going to a company of only two part-
ners and beware of inadvertently failing in some detail. From now on you repeat every day that same
walk and clock in with a strict morning schedule.
Henceforth play fair because the national change so
requests it from you. No rich people games. To
work...

It is the final leg of her errand. High above from the
top of a skeletal sandbox tree there hang two banners
with a red biretta and his wife with a long blond mane
winking mischievously. Look, rain or shine, come
what may, you go out and vote for us to ensure yourself a nice future... *Passing the boat, the boatman
told me, pretty girls do not pay money. I'm not pretty
nor I want to be but my money will not you see...*

For looking up high she fell into the filthy puddle that
invades the entrance of her destination. On all fours,
half blind, full of mud, vanilla and strawberry, she
searches for the point where her journey ends. And it
is hard to find it because plants and vines form a single bunch with the inhabitants of the part. Where
could my beloved torment be?... *Doñana is not here,
she is in the orchard, opening the rose, closing the
carnation....* Oh, oh, now she can see him and she
senses the orgy, seal of the big business.

Gray hair in the wind, wrinkles in the open, she runs
and embeds on his chest, new and polished wood.
They bind, swinging begins... *Sleep my little girl, I*

have to wash the diapers and make food... It is a soft and steady swaying with the wail of hinges, management of shared service. One cannot vibrate without the other; the eternal covenant works- I cannot exist without you- I have wanted this forever- I need your lullaby- I search for you in all the loves.

They pant and she screams. She is born again. Finally clutching her beloved swing.

2

BUT IT IS A SWIRL rocking fasting. Bread, water and salt must nourish the spark that fires up the move.

The next day, in the endless chain of sweating legs that claim for a seat, whether a fragile bench to take turns, there is one common trait. Varicose veins.

And... *who does not venture nothing gains*... sang her father. It is worth enduring this ordeal of heat stroke and fatigue before the celestial and well publicized offer. Hear and see. If you, pleasant radio listener have some free time and want to fill it with a lucrative, dignified and enjoyable activity, do not hesitate to show up. There a single condition. Being a believer.

... *Glory to the brave people*... How was it before? It has been so long – Miss, can we go into the classroom without forming a line? – Teacher, I left the homework at home, but let me in. Professor, I did not bring the book and my uniform is being washed- Teach, do not call the roll, just mark present all of us... And later in college. Professor... *Farmer you are on the land, sailor you are at sea ...Our world of blue berets*... Professor, would you allow us to prolong this discussion? All we are saying is *Give peace a chance*...

Doctor I have to think otherwise, university renewal is the watchword.

For twenty years she could accommodate requests and become supportive of what seemed debauchery because love and interest went to the field one day, and wherever the class time was they went evenly matched, neither could over the other, not in the school nor in the Alma Mater. More and timely enigma and always added. Together with the students, language and literature was a single note.

With scenes of that ilk, there was gestated a bulky dossier that nurtured the wide record that inspired the extensive letter that bid her farewell from each school. Her resume underlined in red pencil ninety percent of the text to avoid the slightest doubt about the impeccable rigor of the complaints and the validity of the beyond suspicion verdict. Expulsion diploma that expresses her credential portrait. Well prepared, ceremonious in gestures, fine speech, seriousness in dressing, recidivist and fractious in her systematic rejection of the application of standards and guidelines of the official program, disrespectful in the violation of plans and methods. The office, supervision and colleagues agree to rate her behavior mythomaniac and puerile. To top it all, she suffers from acute melomania; she usually interrupts a formal class with humorous fables or humming radio music, that is, rude and commercial.

The parchment that enrolled her in a real melancholy after every fleeting achievement. But there was always work, poorly paid, but paid at least.

Now, to stand in line in slow procession with the unemployed is therefore, her specialty. She would be the ideal candidate to preside over an independent union of slackers. Job searching is an exemplary practice to become Job's clone. In a hundred years all bald, is the motto of her headboard.

But a hunch tells her that this time will be different. It is her turn in front of the booth and she passes the good presence test. True to her custom, to feel comfortable and to win the debut test, she wrapped herself in the black suit, starched white blouse like a shirt-cuffs with a well-knotted bow. The cut and color of the unisex smoking allow hiding her belly swollen down to the groin. She hid her venous shins with the wide hem long skirt and thick stockings. And to give it the solemn final touch, she carries on the bun a little mushroom hat that matches the dark matte leather shoes. As for the glasses, she adjusts them behind her ears so they do not slip by the prominent nose because sometimes they dare to slip up her double chin. To top it with a thin rope she drags the cardboard box where she carries her documents of faith, not on the supreme commander of course.

The cashier gives her an envelope addressed to Mrs. Fulgencia in print. It contains a booklet and instructions on how to take to a simple and daily scale the sacrosanct truth. From this moment she is a respectable employed lady, able to promptly pay the cost of a medium rent. She will no longer be a link in that row of hunchbacks and purblinds that behind her prolong the parade of shadows. Who knows if by a secret plan, abuse is synonymous of harass, does it derive from old? Hallucinations?

But the unthinkable occurs. Never before her usual look was more adequate and convenient? She is a peddler of Bibles.

Oh, how sad. There no longer breathes the ingenuity of Don Lino Palacios to countersign that picture with his acute ink of the forties when he drew so much Don Fulgencio, the old gentle and autistic child who had no childhood, secretly in love with Shirley Temple, from there, his Buenos Aires, her perfect idol, and now, who would believe it, her model to reincarnate him as a female clone.

She starts immediately but she adds to the attire a plastic bag filled with the Holy Scriptures. No way she forgets her little doll, this time made of onion paper.

Offering myths, processing prophecies, financing miracles, managing grief and remorse, it is a sublime and daring enterprise that can deliver good dividends of ecstasy. With that in mind she decides to start her new profession for the Buena Estrella lottery stand in her beloved San Jose, and at the door there is a sign that warns: cash today, credit tomorrow yes. – How can I help you, Missus? – Good day. I offer bounded bibles of all types and price – Bibles, you say? – You can buy them in easy installments – And what religion are these bibles from? If you read this one, for example, you have read them all because any of them is not the doctrine of a sect but history of religion. – How is that stuff? – You didn't understand? Not a scrap – don't speak oddly to me? How is it possible that you don't understand me mother? – You are not down to earth, my daughter, that is why I want you to study a practical career – are tormenting me, I don't like Biology, numbers or business – It is a matter of trying, insisting – I am not interested – You should learn a trade, a skill in something concrete so that you can stand up by yourself. You know that when I was a young girl I took a course in basic accounting which has helped me to manage the store, if not, where would we be today? You father is a merchant of chimeras, a person in continuous levitation. That way you will catch up with him soon – I don't wish to be consumed behind a desk like you, caught in a fishbowl, dammit. I can be a teacher, singer, artist, whatever. – When will you see the harsh reality? – But she is flat and very ugly, I love to see lies of beauty – She is hopeless – Did you understand me now sir? Nothing, you talk sweetly, but very confusing. Anyway what I like is Betania and Sorte, you know, the spirits of Jose Gregorio and Maria Lionza and besides the oven is not for buns, although the revolution will supposedly get us out of the hole, would you like a one of those tickets?

Don Avivato, what they call the owner and potential buyer makes an abrupt sign and adds-Time to move on – Please, allow me another little while to show you the wonders of the Arabian Nights, The Decameron and even of the Kama-Sutra which contains a single volume of these, look, you want comedy? Laugh with doddering Sara when Abraham tells her that she will finally get pregnant – Take a listen, peddler Old Horse but backwards, which *Tío* Simon says of...*Loving each other has no schedule or date on the calendar when desires meet...* because a*fter this life there isn't another chance...* ha, ha, it is the real truth, isn't it? Yes man, that love of Master Diaz, from a seventy year old macho for a twenty year old girl, with the plains vernacular lyrics became a hymn almost planetary. In contrast, the old mare will only get, if anything, a sleep cure, payment promise and account closure for lack of funds. Listen Don Avivato, and don't be distracted, if you prefer a good example drama read how Joseph forgave his perverse brothers and praised them without resentment. If what you need is to decipher the key to a profitable economy, analyze the multiplication of loaves and fish that Christ performed. But if what pleases you is crime of passion for adultery you can spy on David and Bathsheba. Oh yes, missy, I saw that on TV during Easter Week.

At each interruption she realizes she is talking to the walls, she lacks the ability to barter, and as her realistic mother envisions, she is good for nothing, but one must insist – Now, if you are looking to outdo yourself, nothing better than the episode of The Ten Commandments, who wrote them? I wasn't Burt Lancaster not Charlton Heston when they took the role of Moses. What matters is how the human spirit sublimated itself there in its aspiration for a civilized coexistence, do you get me? – Look, silence is the best option, the priest's sermons are easier to understand, that's the reason I tell you Missus, give me one of these, I will pay you with lottery tickets, and if the numbers are drawn we will share the prize, fifty-fifty, do you agree?

Episodes of this kind repeat throughout the valley and its surroundings. Dough is no longer enough to travel on a minibus or a jeepney. The torn soles do not prevent her, once the dialogue with the prospective client is exhausted, to kick pebbles and bottle caps, jump a sisal rope and end the task lying on a park bench chatting quietly in front of her altar, the "Avila" park.

33

After that long consultation she goes out ready to find a more modern marketing strategy to place on the market divine voices. It is a difficult task that requires trial and error and a lot of patience. The next day she goes to the boulevard of what was once savannah and large. It seems the adequate stage for a contest of popular and romantic approach, something like a casting for filming that also incites searching for the original story written in the asphalt. For this occasion she puts a touch of rouge on her lips and cheeks just in case someone looks at her. - Guess Miss, what did Adam sing to his Eve... listen... *So much life I gave you that by force you already taste me...* And Solomon to the Queen of Sheba... *It doesn't mean that you have been my only love* ... Sir what did Magdalene tell Jesus... *Love of my loves, blood of my soul...* Isaac to Rebecca... *Anxious to hold you in my arms...*

When that horrible mixture seems to join together they call it kitsch, and the elements that compose it are worth a lot separately. Together they may form a disposable whole false of pretentiousness or conversely, a sophisticated art, a simple look and complex background. The secret demarcation is very thin.

And nothing more relevant than to ramble, limply and, especially now when the people became the sovereign by revolutionary decree, the rough is legal, legitimate and negotiable, the homeland a speech of chained melodrama and the changes, pushes to equalize crushing toward the basement, equalizing downwards. But the passer of that commercial sector does not seek political analysis or riddles, no one wants a vagrant prima donna singing nicely but rather peddler cards because trade is a sin, says the president.

At sunset she slumps into a concrete chair on the edge of the promenade for walkers, and at dawn she goes by bus to the office of her employer located in an industrial zone, is it the reason it reeks of polluting poison? She has a proposal she is sure he will love – Mr. Manager for that merchandise which initial capital is the forever and ever sacred legacy I would like to set out... Sorry to interrupt you ma'am, we were about to call you to notify you about a virtual menu of broad scope, because today it is the most effective showcase with the support of an eight hundred number opening a survey for Internet users. Here is the printed brochure that will soon appear on our website but that you should start promoting at a very low cost. I can read you a few lines in advance, listen. Do you think Scarlet, Delilah, Jezebel and Salome are heroines? Do you like that our creator remains alone and in need of praise? Was Noah right betraying friends and brothers to save himself and his clan? Must we abide by the supreme authority that commands you to sacrifice your family, as almost had to do the obedient Abraham with his son Isaac?

The spacious pavilion of the boss is lined with a string of images and pictures that accumulate chaotically. Impresses that bunch of saints and miracle workers in the cell of their   gilded moldings.

Making faces she expresses boredom- I already understood Mr. Fortunato Rueda, I am not dumb, tell me, you profess some special religious belief, I guess – But it is a brilliant strategy, I continue, listen. Was it lawful that Jacob tricked Esau to steal his birthright? Did you know that the same patriarch Jacob is the ancestor in direct line of the David-Joseph-Jesus dynasty. Did you know that Saul and Samuel executed the genocide of the Amalekites by holy command?

She then remembers her youthful reading of atheistic philosophers and doubts that she poses on wind instruments that in the mouth of a few musicians shredded Jericho and the merciless punishment for the pious Job, also, it doesn't seem reasonable that the construction of the First temple is assigned to the wise Solomon overloaded with effort with seven hundred wives and three hundred concubines. There's even who notes that not a few of these unions were only a political pact, because if not where is the crowd of children that resulted from mating so many times? Maybe not such a super macho was the poet king.

But she feels dazed by Rueda's chatter, she covers her ears and jumps from the chair screeching – This is net kitschy for canning. Stop, shut up, enough, I get it –

Yes, I am about to finish, it is something from another world, very interesting Missus, isn't it? – Of course, very provocative, but I smell plagiarism, besides, who can answer those sharp questions already has at least two versions of the Old and New Testaments – You are partially right, at first glance it seems a wrong target but it is not because advertising in these terms is controversial and promotes the growth of sales among those who know the product only by references, do you follow me? – Like a swindle of cerebral aspect. Let me tell you, sir, that in private I enjoy this little trick but not to sell it – Now she turned out to be leftish, or communist, it doesn't matter, better, it is fashionable and it sells.

She sits down again. She recounts the beatified, relics and symbols of various cults hanging there and wants to finish with the burden. – Look, it is not necessary that you expel me, I am leaving this troupe because even if you decide that the promotion is partially electronic, I dread imagining the overwhelming power of a machine invented by man, it would leave unemployed, rank or control the all mighty powerful engineer we call God, the mystical breath that by chance or will founded this wonderful universe.

Watching at the sarcastic expression of the editor, marked contrast to his austere conventional looks – graying beard and mustache, vest and Scottish type jacket – she emptied the duffel bag placing twenty bibles on the managerial desk, she hid her little paper fetish in a pocket, distended her muscles, sighed and said in a loud tired voice – Here is the bag with its values. But before leaving, I would like to tell you a medieval legend, if you allow me – I can spear five minutes, I have a very punctual board of directors meeting – I will be as fast as you have been. You should hear. Once certain wise man produced a puppet in human form, he breathed life through formulas learned in the Kabbalah and it was so perfect, that he decided to use it as a substitute servant. He called him Golem and was his slave for many years. One dark night of apocalypse that arrogant creature of sawdust and glue used the confident dream of his father to shatter him by the same means that he had been engendered. So Mr. boss, hungry and thirsty and calluses on the feet, not for all the gold in the world I will stop fishing fables, illusion and delusion in the net that allows this navigation. I really appreciate the opportunity to earn my sustenance. But do not expect me to burn in your monetary and electric bacchanal the lyrical and sensory orgasm of the Song of Songs... *Beneath the shadow of the desired I sat down, and its fruit was sweet to my taste, it led me to the banquet hall and its flag over me was love, nourish me with raisins, comfort me with apples, because I am faint with love ...* Neither the treatise on human frailty that David poeticized with the sound of the harp in the

Psalms... *Behold, how good and pleasant it is for brethren to dwell together in harmony...* and I give you another verse... *I am like a pelican of the wilderness, like the owl of solitudes...* Holy crap Missus, can you tell me who you really are? – *I am what Hillel said, if you knew, very much admired by Jesus, pay attention. If I do not do it for me, who will do it. But if I don't commit myself to myself, who shall do it? And if not now, when.* Don't worry, neither Catholic, nor apostolic and Roman and much less red, but there is no cash in the bank that tempts me to sully the bright parables and allegories conceived by the poet Jesus of Nazareth... *Blind guides, who strain out a gnat and swallow a camel...* And the other one... *No, lest gather up the tares you also root up the wheat with them.* Let both grow until the harvest... I guess you've at least heard about... *The spirit is always willing, the flesh is weak...* That who am I? Find out, but even under torture I will be screwing the plot of this inexhaustible file of intellect, sex and emotion without time that I could not sell a single copy, the clearest mirror of the garbage and grandeur we are. I'm sorry Mr. Director, I see you have no idea of what I am talking about. You at least do your business directly and so anything goes. But there are thousands who cheat using their position and appearance as Secretaries of whom they call the Highest. Forgive me for making you the scapegoat of this singsong rancor of long standing.

Her blood rhythm has cut loose. Pulse of burning rumba in Cuban son and counterpoint jam-jazz fever in New Orleans- Good-bye then, pal. I am also in a hurry. On Fridays, at six o'clock I begin to desecrate my sacrum and seventh day. Respect the glow of my bible hidden for centuries to prevent people like you, who doesn't respect itself and wants to burn the mysticism and the people who do not think like you just to fill their pockets with ash.

As she heads toward the exit, she opens her black jacket, unbuttons the while blouse, takes off her shoes, dishevels, at the rhythm of hips and hands in the snapping of castanets she recites the last Psalm... *Praise him to the tune of the horn, with tambourine and dance, with strings and flutes, with cymbals of joy...*

Perhaps the hanging Santeria in that damn office of tricks, she rolled very stunned with the door slamming that reverberated even in the sewers of the earth and heaven.

3

AT THE MEMORY OF HER FAILURE as dealer of bibles she is enveloped by that nostalgia that being chronic already has a title and she stole it from a touching Duke Ellington composition... *It shouldn't happen to a dream*... and it seems invented for both she and the *gringa*....

With no possibility of escape, the daily sustenance is a siege. Will I have to sign up with the red party to eat? Among the economic classified ads, one stands outs as an intruder. Okay. Due to inventory and change of activity we are liquidating everything at absurd discounts, from a safety pin to a Jacuzzi. Don't believe in promises, only our people can meet their most pressing needs. Okay. The madness is for thirty-six hours, until Sunday. Okay. We are expecting you. Okay.

Well, it will be the only way of getting certain basic consumer goods. At the bottom of the dirty clothes basket, wrapped in a thin washcloth, there appears her piggy bank, pink heart with a visible opening. The small key is an enigma that she will solve at the right time. She presses the base and coins start coming out through its wide slot. How many memories... Mom, the chicha seller is here, I'm running to the other corner, I took some of the money from my piggy bank, money I'm saving to buy the doll. – What doll are you talking about? – You know, Lulu, the one that opens and closes her eyes and has clothes to dress her. – Here are your little sisters to do the same without having to buy anything, but when I ask you to change their diapers, you grumble, – It is not the same, mom – Uh-huh, since you are going out, go to the bodega and bring me... Oh, no, what a pain! – How you dare interrupting your elders? Here you have a Fuerte, buy one Bolivar of meat for soup, another of a compound of herbs, real and a quart of ground corn, and twenty five cents of sea salt. With the other half... – Jeez, more? – Little brat. Go to the busses garage and ask for a real of kerosene to be brought in a closed can, and add a loach of matches – And why don't you send Petra? Her trade is washing and ironing, and I have already told you that you must learn the value of money and keep track of it – Can I buy some goodies? – Only for two cents. Bring me back the rest complete, and not even one cent must be missing, beware – Can I spare the rest and this way I can gather more money to get Lulu soon? – I gave you precise orders – You are so miser, I am going to tell my daddy – Your father and I made sacrifices so that you eat the best food and study in the best school. Toys and spoiling you are extravagances for when there are plenty of savings. The day you earn your own living you will spend without being held accountable.

And it is to enjoy the privilege of living happily that she browses anxiously around the many stores of the giant bazaar. Maybe the primary objects that will lead her to paradise are not sold out. She shoves her way through here – Get out of the way, old fart – that is all the time. It is good luck that she can hear her only some of those compliments, because the noise in the mall is deafening. Half an hour later she comes out carrying a huge package that almost crushes her and she does not let it go on the escalator or in the subway. Today she suffers that acute *Terredad* written by Eugenio Montejo... *Straight scaffolds, tower on tower, now they hide the mountain...*

The date is convenient she still has shelter. In a few days, and no excuses, she will have to leave her hideout because the workers, flat out, are renewing and ending with the oasis of her room, drilling fountains and stones. A flow of moisture and debris is choking her and covers her with a rash.

She has to prepare the oil. Grab the present and keep in mind that the preparations require care to detail. Note that it is noon and the nocturnality is achieved with the blinds closed. Remember; leave a crack to watch the bright green of your hill. Freshen the environment with the essence of the sprayer that spreads flowery field smells. She rips the wrapping of the

43

snacks placed on the coffee table by the vase with the purple roses, places her bottle of scotch, her glass, her ice bucket, do not forget the napkins and the cigarette box with the lighter, double check.

On the side table, to your right, you place the device with the cassette within range. Check out the plugs to make sure that a blackout will not leave you holding the bag. The section of the corner cabinet is for her slippers, her burgundy silken gown, lavender, comb, toothbrush, shaving cream and pads.

Don't forget, for starters you offer him a drink with the famous blue pill so that in a while his vision stops in a diffuse fog, slightly bluish, and his virility holds for several hours. The package of condoms, Egyptian brand should not be visible because it breaks the spell of this atmosphere. Extend the armchair before the television.

You did it. With such great care, this *garçonniere* that will soon be called apartment only for executives has the ambience of a mini-*boite*. Here he comes. Come in darling.

–All alone at last, my love. Your punctuality reflects that last night you stayed awake thinking about me, thanks. That's what happened to me when you appeared in my life for the first time and I fell in love at first sight. I didn't want to find out your age, marital status, number of children and lovers, fortune or fame.

44

And you? My dear friend. The heat associated with this celebration obliges me to ask you a question, listen well, *How was it? I cannot tell you how it was, I cannot explain myself what happened, but I fell in love with you...* Exactly, but I would tell you that you turned me on, I drooled, nothing more. If you had asked me, I would go with you to an aparthotel or behind a screen, anywhere. And you, what did you like about me? – *Were your eyes or your mouth; were your hands or your voice? It was perhaps the impatience waiting for your arrival, I just don't know...* Look, how the talent of Benny More and Graciela Naranjo make theirs and ours this beautiful bolero whenever they sing it, right? Now, my adorable little friend; would you like a cornerstone of love at first sight? Listen to it then... *Suddenly as the child that becomes a teenager, as one goes crazy and confuses his past and present...* Literally, it may be true that in love we do not choose, we are captivated, since I heard you, since I felt you... *Suddenly, you took away the wrinkles of my forehead and you sow your smile in my pain...* Oh, to fall in love... a total rebirth. When this is over I don't even want to think. Darling, hey center all your attention in this ballad, the classical oath of undying love. *I will never leave your life and neither will you from my heart, although destiny takes us to different ways that matter to us both...* – That you say now, but everything that begins ends, and in a man like you, this leaves no footprint – *I have you within my soul, as a sun tattoo, and in my veins throbs the flame of your heart....*

The preamble precipitates. She, fiery, impatient, passionately cuddles his manly chest. He, calm and always under control, observes her fearsome outburst.

And then, she desperately unbuttons his shirt an fly, unties his tie and lunges... Help me, I'm crying help me, I can't hold it anymore... hug, nobody is looking at us, don't feel troubled or afraid, no one will come...

Explodes the dynamo that opens a hole to remodel the construction. He with his wise voice, cuts the frenzy of her total submission – Yes, loving, listen up, in every couple there is always one more vehement, law of love, it is written, from that comes the wounded hearts. – Of course, *it is easy to be loved as I am loving you, but I don't know if I want to give you what the heart yearns. I offer you...* – Well, we are approaching the half time, time thief also for lovers, check it with this melodic poem... *After we kissed, with soul and life, you left with the night of that farewell...* People say that man is fire, the woman is tow, the devil comes and blows. Not always. Her rapture is lubricated without blood or semen, only with vagina fluid, sweat and tears... *We are two drops of tear in a song... That is all we are, nothing mooore...* Well lovely woman it is time..*We have to bid farewell, because maybe never ever, I will find you again*... Beautiful ending, right? Thank you for listening to this session of boleros, a special of Daily Bolero celebrating Valentine's Day. Don't forget to tune in again tomorrow, at the same time. – But, how can you think that I ever forget to listen to your program if I have always been hearing the tone of your voice, since I was a schoolgirl wearing ankle socks and would skip classes not to miss a single one. Those fifteen minutes of bolero are a fixed point in my daily journal and my hot line, live or recorded because you are my perpetual boyfriend. Mind you, I will never meet you in person, although I wish it with all my heart and soul, and as the wise saying... If you fall in love with the voice of the speaker, don't go to the station...

She presses the off button and removes the tape. The volcanic coterie has concluded passion to measure. The life size mannequin, lean and tanned, with his curly jet black hairpiece as she likes, returns to its box. – Don't lose your composure, dear, I'm your Satin Doll and you are my Barbiu. And for the trust between us, allow me to change, this performance has left me exhausted.

Said and done, she takes off all the removable. The curly red haired wig, the padded push-up bra, the mesh pantyhose, the buckle and gold strips platforms, the negligee, one by one, the makeup of the trousseau are falling on the worn-out carpet.

Early, during the shopping of that eventful morning, in digital technology, which is the magnet department of the macro store, she wanted to buy a video-robot on a human scale, a brain of silicone full of circuits forging artificial intelligence, those that are about to reach even the own wishes. But she needed it malleable and of high plasticity, with a wireless mouse for her to direct its movements and rictus. But even the hourly lease contract has an unpayable cost. And since beggars can't be choosers, she opted for this plastic nacre figurine that can somewhat move eyebrows, mouth and fingers. Also maneuverable from the ball of his own mental cable.

She confesses she was scared. She thought this lifeless cutie, glowing as a toff, would be unable to fulfill his task. No way! That quiet attitude, love receiver, allows that as always, manipulating, she fulfills his jack of all trades role, and also for that, his habitual selection, the alien and passive, is believed to be quite real, almost human.

Horseplay operetta? Sugary drama? Mock science-fiction?

Realizing it. It is amazing the splendor that can create the minutiae of the décor in a room, how real can masquerade be, including the current government, including the morbid glamour to touch precipice depths.

And she realizes it. Although life is beautiful, still some son of the Holocaust settles the miracle of half-surviving with the purpose of... *This bolero is mine...* An affliction in blues and games at a loss. But much further back, there whines a withered child, yes, still an old creature.

Either way, impeccably finishes the Fitzgerald... *This should not happen to a dream...* Never.

4

SHE AWAKES WEARIED due to yesterday's performance. It is urgent that she goes to the park again and sits on her swing that releases her so much.

But it is not possible. Who knows through which crack there slipped a striking envelope that haunts her. At a glance she wants it to be an affiliation card to the social service that protects the well behaved idlers. It seems rather an elegant wedding invitation. Nonsense. From its first line it is very far from the pleasant heading, Dear Mrs. – You must appear within the allotted time at the precise place, to meet the commitment made before witnesses appointed based on their honorability. By mandate of the board of directors you are notified that failure to comply with this latter request, the institution, applying rules and regulations that constitute it, will be forced to terminate the agreement. The consequences are your sole responsibility for having failed...

Oh, divine sun, blessed art thou painter who from dawn can make up this hill of silky grass, always Avila, I am longing of this greenish in every shade. Now I am prevented by... you have to... you must... *We owe the tree caring love...* They are looking for her as a criminal, the police come with an arrest warrant, she may end up in jail. It is an abuse. What law states how am I going to spend my day and my night. Human rights, where are they?

She indeed made a rather pious deal and for playing dumb for a few weeks, first time, they redact this flyer that humiliates her. In which code does it say they can force you to eat, sleep, defecate and stay in that horrible penitentiary. Hey, wake up, stretch, recharge your corporal battery because... *The meeting is at six; don't forget about me, so many things I want to tell you...*

Who knows, perhaps she might solve her homelessness if she stays quiet and nerveless in that kindergarten that only admits droopy kiddies using magnifying glasses and canes. But just at looking from afar its facade, she turns and is Judy Garland, with her very red shoes and thick braids hanging down to the skirt that reaches above the knees, she goes for a walk with the Wizard of Oz to sing about the rainbow and to ask the Tin Man – Why do you look so afflicted? – I want faith, charity and hope, longing those yearnings. But I don't have, I lack the heart – Come then, see, let's find it.

Old folk's home... vomits and homesickness.

–Why do you condemn me to be here? – It is necessary, there are doctors, nurses – I'd rather die – This

decision comes from above, be thankful and no claims
– Then, where will I protest, in the cemetery?

She knows she is a scoundrel and she can't be helped, she deserves the scolding of the citation. For many long months she forgot the agreement with the authorities of the nursing home, she ignored the visits and abandoned Reina Perales, the sole vestige of her huge kinsfolk. Let's see if you can pretend to listen with respect and play along with her. After all   it is good deed for a while, every thirty days. Not much sacrifice to show amazement at her talk, which you know by heart. – Listen and look my little one, good smell is the study and good taste the good deeds. Do not try to be like the myrtle with only a smell, as the date with flavor only, and less like the willow that does not satisfy either the smell or the taste buds. One should look like the lemon that tastes and smells good.

Or the other. Oh, you came Fulgencia, the Messiah came, a guest of honor. – Forgive me, I had problems Yes, you broke up with the guy – Who told you? Bad news travel fast, hah, hah – Your friend's filthy tongue of course – And it was known that you visited him in his office – If you live locked up within these four walls, how do you find out what happens in the city? Comments are that you have been left alone That was ages ago – Yesterday. On any date dear, obeys a fixed rule that does not expire –One more? Never seek or chase the man, even if he is your fiancé, your husband. – Goodness gracious, a lady of your level, who came to such a primitive land, wad to raise children, helped her husband, colleagues for fifty years, having a gift for languages, reads and perceives everything but is so slow in these matters. – I'm talking from my experience, I learn from nature – This the way you call it now? It's a natural law. If you observe the behavior of animals, from the ant to the elephant, you see that if the male takes the initiative and desires the female, it overcomes all obstacles to get her. – And the queen bee? – Funny case and confirms the rule because it ends up alone, right? Aha, and what else? That if it is the other way around, it always ends badly.

Clothing, hair and eyebrows as Marlene Dietrich, dry gums, dentures that slide down the wheelchair in each phrase, alert gaze, her hands fly.

The parents' villa of - drool and sighs.

Psyche chat – You have a medieval mentality, typical of the frustrated and resigned woman. – No Miss, we as mothers have a squishy soul, we are compassionate and we know how to solve problems. At first, you may not feel passionate love but if this man insists, we accept at the end. If he loves us and has good feelings, it wills work – Mom, stop it. This is a male chauvinist world because ladies like you would make the bed and set the table. – What right do parents have to direct their children in love decisions? – what you call love will come with cohabitation. You are a governess as the ones described by Charles Dickens in his stories. – I don't know much about literature. What I like is tally, not tales.

Today she is more elegant than ever. While she chats, her companion wearing a neat white uniform fixes her makeup, changes her soaked diaper, bathes her in cologne and arranges the pillows to hold her straight up, because as in The Blue Angel, she aims at subjugating her interlocutor with posture and a direct stare of controlled seduction.

She does not stop. – If the woman loves too much and harasses, he might end up accepting in appearance. Either if she is a saint or a call girl, the couple will stay together until he wants. That is the great secret – My God, how long will I have to endure this Dick Tracy in a skirt, an apron and holding a gavel? There is no way you let me live my life – Stand your ground, there are too many good catches out there, you are very young, attractive and capable – Speak, my mother, how incredible, so prepared and heeding to gossiping of those wastrel, envious and jealous women. – On the contrary, it is for your own good, someday you will acknowledge that I am right – Never, how dare you…

She was right... *I like you and you, and you, and only you, I care about you and nobody else*... It is Carmencita's boyfriend, he doesn't even know I exist, he never asks me to dance in the record playing parties, I love so much Billo's guarachas... *There come the cadets in perfect formation*... and the slow one... Great *Swing and Son. It is not bolero, rumba or danzon*... Alfonzo Larrain's boleros are fantastic, fabulous... *Stop looking at me*... that's a lie, don't take your eyes off of me, ask me and let's dance cheek to cheek this song, the theme of Larrain's orchestra does not have lyrics but it contains all the passionate unreason to hold on tightly, and they play it exactly as the North American bands that one hears on the radio. And you, my real true Tony Curtis; do you know I am your student? Instead, I... *For someone like you I would*... learn by heart the phone book of the twenty states, two territories and the Federal District, the peaks of the Andes and even the catalog of the battles that Bonaparte won and recite them to you in the oral exam, as long as you look at me at least for a second... *I don't know what is wrong with me, but I have to tell you*... you are identical to the guy holding on his shoulders the globe on the cover of the atlas for the sophomore year.

Oh yeah, right, but I do not exist because I am a flat board, nothing on the front, nothing on the back or the sides, ha ha. If my classmates say so is because they understand well the subject. Then of course, he only has eyes for Isabelita that she doesn't even know her ABC's but she sits in the front row, very demure she pulls up the blue uniform so that he can see her panties and her navel, in the middle of the moral an civics class. Do I shut up? Do I confess?

The following and ten years later, she will follow him with her eyes and red cheeks, a meter from her trembling hands, every Thursday evening during the seminar on history of culture, oops, she is attracted by that mouth with thick mustache and that Harry Belafonte color – But would you marry someone like him? – Like what? – C'mon girl *negrito tinto*, wirehaired – I 'll answer when I graduate but for now I'd love to go out with him, let him squish me as we dance in a new place around Chacaíto where they say Aldemaro Romero plays piano, imagine – You are crazy – Why? – First of all because, he likes big Creole women – Dumb, do you suppose someone is fu or tope only for their favorite color? And you intend to be a lawyer of the republic? – It's for his habits, people – Yellow, blue or red... *May the sky run out of stars and the wide sea lose its immensity, but the black of his eyes should not die and the cinnamon color of his skin stays the same...* Should I drop a handkerchief as a Marguerite Gautier or am I Marilyn Monroe with bare tits and ass? Do I sing to him in *With a song in my heart* kind

56

of a Doris Day or should I claim... *What did I ask you for?*... tearing up my clothes as La Lupe weeps?

Living space of the elder... complaints and urine.

I beg you to hear me Fulgi, I hear you Reina, mother and aunt, how well you look, as seductive as always, our Lilly Marlene. Let it be so 'till one hundred twenty – Oh no, please, don't wish me that. God gave you humans only twenty years did you know? But it happened that beasts had a conference and it seemed to them unfair that short life, then they decided to give each one a certain portion of theirs That's why after turning twenty, man works like a donkey, swallows like a pig, runs back and forth like a horse and jumps like a monkey, ha ha, but me, I am fixed here without going out... – You have always been very active but here they do wonders for your rheumatism, your bronchitis, your asthma, your intercostal neuritis, your insomnia, your heartburn, your infections... – I wish to live and die for my taste – Here you have a beautiful garden, you can enjoy closely the green of the Avila, and across the street a few old trees – Yes, I also became a tree, I wet myself inadvertently, the breeze cradles me, the little birds chirp at me, I hear the dew falling and some throw stones at me, hardly anyone looks at me... Paradise for the disabled... furies and poop.

– Girl. You're not listening to me, don't look me in the eyes, then why do you visit me – I hear every

57

word, I like to look at you and I say with your admired Madame Coco Chanel, a woman is as old as she deserves to be.

So it was during the university round table on poetry and revolution, he only deigned to look at her askance as she reads her essay on the two Juanas poetesses , the Mexican Sister Agnes and the modern from Uruguay. He so leftist, congratulates her with charro smile – what tomfoolery, wasting the brain, burning the midnight oil with that shit rather than delving into key issues for these cyclical changes ahead? – Such as? – The Commitment of the artist, naked popular expression, naïf painting, motivations abound... *I would like to be the first purpose of your life and be in you, in the same way you are in me, represent in your life the sun, emotion, faith, and that emotion of love that one only lives oooonce...*

Sure, Rosa Virgina Chacin, I want to be all that for him and sing sweetly and convincingly as you do, but, you know, why do I have to kneel down? What right does that small group of ideologues, Party members and bunglers have to manage my tastes, interests and my curriculum? He pays attention when I speak and write, well, I believe in this and they call the bourgeois right but I rent in a dilapidated building in San Jose, he believes in other extreme the east, gee, that's his thing, but If he lives at a mansion in the exclusive south, can we respect our cardinal points and also make out? Because let me tell you... *The woman that does not peek at love doesn't deserve to be called woman...* that's as true as *The Capital*, and if the good-looking Alfredo Sadel makes it clear to you, undoubtedly with great knowledge of the facts... *The woman has a magical language that in between kisses one must learn...* Do you hear comrade? You think I'm a siren and the scales cover me from the neck ,you don't even desire my lips, only my intellect and to mold it to your needs you ask me for words, I can give exclusively... *Three words are my anxieties... And those words are, how I like you...*

Thanks for coming, Alondra, your real name, you are cheerful like that little bird, they call you Fulgita, you are very decent – True, Reina, I'm still pretty virgin – Of course, and you'll be well rewarded, believe me, it is true... *Loves one has in life are never forgotten, they are flavors that stay in the air and a trail of fragrances they leave...* You make fun of me, you always have your head in the clouds, singing all day long, and that is since you were a little girl but I know you, now you sing not to answer my question – This beautiful song was composed by Ilan meaning tree, always in bloom – Not like me huh? Without stems or fruit... But it's because rooted trees have little foliage... – Uproot me from this prison, my daughter, I want to be a housewife, cooking, have my housekeeper, I worked, I saved for old age here I'm neither alive or dead who

59

has the right to say where I put down roots, they, you or me? They're the rules of life... You're right, you put the preferred sign but it still is a Jurassic Park live and direct. Dying place of little singing and lots of crying. One has to... you have to... one must...i t is mandatory... Reina is right, very much so, she cannot move the legs but she kicks.

In the good old days, Uncle Tiger, Uncle Rabbit, Cockroach Martinez and Mouse Perez further back than ever, the first story she was told during a family feast, that once upon a time there was a father of four children that were praying during that feast of the Easter night, and he said that this was different from the other nights because one must comply with the law, celebrate it every year, then the wise son questioned – What are we celebrating today? The wicked asked – And you, what are you remembering? – The simpleton – What is being celebrated? And the ignorant that didn't know what to ask, that one had to be explained in detail the reason for the dinner. Very difficult for little kids, but my dad told it year after year. There must have been a reason because now she understands the story, ancient narrative bridge for generations which insists you must fight each and every day to be free since bondage is above all ignorance, then mourn and bitter herbs – Never forget that once you were a slave and never what to be again even if they call you rebel without a cause.

Mansion of the fragrant old man... Yes, the old lady smells good, but her perfume of exquisite brand fails to dispel that dungeon bad breath choking with its sick medicinal steam. Well, she complied with the standard. Her family duty as daughter, niece. She regrets oblivion. Luckily now she doesn't need to go in person to the oratory to ask for forgiveness of the sins, there already are religions, on the net and you are absolved of blame by simply clicking a button of the computer suitable for this crucial rite. What a pity. Her temple is invisible, secret and keeps her prayers in a particular limbo. From now on she will fulfill it. She doesn't want to receive another summons and yes my aged madam, stay there in accordance with regulations. Aging one enjoys better childhood friends.

How wonderful it would be a long life as willowy button that just doesn't blossom and as an immature fruit that never rots, always green. Is that why in each trance, leaving the mandatory asylum she is a bird of different plumage. Once she was Madonna, in contortion of the face, arms and feet. Another time, there danced Isadora Duncan among shawls. Last time, maybe because she was wearing a t-shirt and her little doll on the shoulder, she was a light fairy on extremely high heels and dreams inside a colossal tent of acrobats and she left with the Cirque du Soleil.

Today, wearing sandals and shorts, she is a tree, standing on. Who knows if this refuge can also survive firm the new regime.

It is known that the continuous transplant of the vine seeks soils that improve the flavor of the grapes. And that by itself, the almond tree blossoms even in winter, but she chooses to be an olive tree. Because the olive never wrinkles, takes green year round and doesn't lose its leaves. When someone cuts a branch, puts it in a pigeon's peak, it is to say peace.

5

THE HOURS THAT FOLLOW that monthly grace always become sleepless and prolonged night. Such tiredness. From the huge event planning agency there comes a murmur of a marriage procession broken by the renovating drill rammed in the corridors of the building from which she has to move out... *I got married, I am in a jam, I have a husband and a mother-in-law as well*... was the cockiness of Tannhauseer that mocks outwitting Richard Wagner chanted in the bachelorette parties. But it cannot share any amusement that turns grotesque the relationship of the genders. I would prefer a thousand times to mutter. I already have the little house that I promised, and full of daisies, for you, for me... Now we will be happy. Now we can sing that song that goes like this, with its tropical rhythm, lalala...

Copulation in love, that intimate mutual surrender, had to be a delight in a private alcove and unfit for jocks or mocks – God after creating man, would not leave him alone. Adam awoke, recognized Eve as the flesh and bones of his own and decided that with her they would become one body, leaving the house of the father and mother... That's what descants the officiating tenor at that ceremony in the synagogue, emotion that followed the one at the civil registry. And adds with melody... *The blessings only become true when married couple is lying together and get to know each other...*

– What's going on? Mom and dad are not talking, not even discussing, not even a pin drop can be heard – That is very strange. And the door of the bedroom is locked from the inside, how strange, should we knock – That's insane, girl, don't even think about it. When our parents don't speak, read, cry, laugh and especially not argue, is because they are making love or already asleep. We better be quite enough!

Certainty and fixed portrait. There was also a staging repeated ad nauseum with slight variations. Dad surrounds mom's shoulders and looking at her slyly – Do you know something daughters? If it weren't for the evil inclination I feel for this lady, I would not have embarked, or gotten married, you would not be there watching us, or I would not work killing myself. It means that this evil is very good right? – How horrible, do not talk about those things in front of the girls, you're a foul-mouthed, go ,go, get your books, play your mandolin and let me educate them. You are wrong – so, what's new? It's great that they hear and see us because the Saturday of peace, the brilliance of the sun and sex are the three lines that form the semblance of heaven; so say the sacred writings, not me.

So, my lady, scold those who wrote that, not me, I'm an illiterate, ha ha.

By some hidden impulse and even if it were the fiftieth time they laughed at the parental joke, among pounding beats she evoked... *When I return to your side, and be alone with you, the things I tell you, never repeat them* ... engraved on her hard drive and accepts that she can only get together in bed eroticism with initial advances... *In a sentimental mood...*

But everything must come to an end. Doctor, what's wrong with my husband? I've summoned urgently the family to ask you a lot of mettle. My patient needs special care – What is it, what's wrong with Dad? – First, He is seventy-five years old with the addition of a disease that attacks and destroys the brain, fatal memory loss and other nerve functions. Eventually he will be an old baby and will need exclusive attention day and night – What does that mean? Someone to feed him, tidy him up, move him, interpret his silence and babbling, dry his tears and help him walk. His other self – That someone will be me, doctor. No lady, the caretaker of such a sick person should be someone alien to these terrible emotions that this progressive deterioration causes him and his immediate family. You, especially, should move to another site, near, but separate to preserve your health – Are you crazy? Where did you go to college? I will stay beside in sickness and even death; I do not discuss the subject

65

with anyone. Only over my dead body I will accept that nurses bury him alive, how much do I owe you? I'll walk you to the door. And you guys listen, I'm warning you, I volunteered because I do not accept anyone else taking care of my husband, is that clear? *... I offer you to be the joy of my life, that you inspire every night a song you're my eternal partner in crime...*

Forgetfulness is in principle a flash, in Spanglish. But on the contrary, it is an impression, deep scar, fatal when attacking villages and is already, happening right now because young people do not know their history. Could be erased this new evil perhaps with a high power detergent, laser beams, lotions to undo indelible marks. It requires great, great resistance...

By the flowing of these footprints inside, Mendelssohn's wedding march in the distance and the soil driller so close, the phone ringing is added. It is Goldy Oropeza, retired actress, pensioner and a fan of soap opera, friend forever, tone and rhythm in strict order – Fulgita what about you? I call, call and never find you, you are no spring chicken. I want you to participate in the workshop and competition for *telenovela* scripts, it is a valid option if you want to abandon the cajolery, get timely payment and safe housing. And I pay for the registration, I do not accept excuses. Go, get dressed, the course starts at five in the afternoon and less of your tales okay?... *To my friends I will give*

when I die, my devotion in a guitar chord, and among
the forgotten verses of a poem, my cicada poor incor-
rigible soul...

Here she is in the famous television station, breathing
through the large window on the fourth floor an Avila
of pink and violet with traces of blue and while, together with a dozen of middle aged, aspiring to con-
cord exciting plots, see their names on the screen
credits and maximum rating programs.

She brought as support, a white fluffy bunny, identical to the one wearing a checkered vest, cane, and
pocket watch created by Lewis Carroll when he invented his wise declaration of love for the girl Liddell,
her English half-homonym of the eighteen hundreds,
And advised by the prudent, mundane Goldyale, she
disguised herself and looks like a reliable person. She
is wearing her beige corduroy suit, scarf and heeled
loafers. And at the lack of a female briefcase, her always new mahogany portfolio that she uses since
high-school. She has a youthful bang and holds the
graying strands with the tortoiseshell comb. She
doesn't manage to be revolutionary but yes, still has
flirtatious.

Opening the course the young professor Ivan Espejo
requests the identification cards of those attending,
reason and synopses of each proposal. When he re-
views the documents he shakes the manila folder and

pointing with his index finger – Missus Fulgencia, excuse me, we asked you for a front photograph card size, and of course yours, is this baby your daughter or your granddaughter? Oh, forgive me, with the rush I gave you my own photo that I always carry with my documents. When I get this oblivion attacks, I look at it and remember whom I am, where I go, so I don't lose my way, do you understand?

An oppressive silence of suppressed laughter goes from wall to wall – Did you bring the summary requested? – it just occurred to me. While we waited, I read in the newspaper about this boy, the endless comic strip *Blondie and Dagwood* and I thought, gee, there's no better argument than observing the yester-year experiences with the eyes of today. That couple, the Bumstead, I have known them since I was a little girl and spelled – Who are they? – Look, the young wife, blond curls, Bibelot face, went from being a knucklehead, to a model matron with clothes bought on sales, even when she goes into the tub she is coiffed, covered and revived, for sure, her husband's bigwig. He, a disinherited playboy who became a very middle class cliché husband, black suit, red bow tie, mop of hair hanging on both sides of his forehead and popping eyes – Could they be Pepita and Lorenzo? – Created by Chic Young. I guess no one has yet discovered the business of the office where he receives a salary so low he could never buy even a used car and will continue being a stow away on the roof of buses and trams – What is the story? – Pay attention, he stays too long at home fulfilling the useless tasks she assigns him and culminates in severe hardship on the couch. He is the domestic obedient lazy bones – What drew you to this stupidity? – What do you mean? World-class brains, encyclopedias and monographs analyze this phenomenon you know? There are even those who believe that Lorenzo's endless nap is a defense buffer against fierce matriarchy. Let me also tell you that this comic strip has been translated into most of the world languages, has a calculated audience of hundreds of millions, inspired twenty films, a novel, and so you know, a TV series – I still can't distinguish a storyline, where do you attend Mass? – That a while ago I had a bad scare. In the seven squares of the sequence published today, the incredible is announced. – What could it be? – A couple's crisis that breaks that apparent loggerhead atmosphere –Please detail the process – Alright. Frame one. Pepita well-dressed to leave home says I need to make sure I did not forget anything. Two Daisy, the dog, has water and food. – Three All the windows are closed. Four – I think that's all... Daisy, windows, lights... Yes, I'm sure that's all .But, oh surprise, in the fifth frame, behind the front window of the house there is a cry Pepita! Pepita! She, from the sidewalk, dazed – Heavens! What did I forget?

Pay attention colleagues. Sixth and last. Lorenzo finally appears agitated as usual, desperate, eyes about to pop out, shrieking – "Me!" What is new in this ridiculous story? something very serious. For some time she is not at home full-time, she ceased being the domestic geisha and works as a businesswoman in her own fast food business do you follow me? – And? Time is running out Sirs, – Her furniture is antique but the pressure changes, the tension between spouses can be felt – Where do you want to get – I still don't know but in this synthesis once and for all I give you everything you asked me for, the subject, description of characters, their physical typology and psychological set. The decor should be specified, the ambience certainly, as if it were a vaudeville ... – And the turning points for your project to be fairly acceptable? This is not a hobby but a serial novel technique that requires some skill, even minimal, to attempt it – That's why I'm here, but in my draft Pepita arises several vital issues. Do you want to persist in the marital style she favored? Is she still virtuous, taking profit from frailties, rescuing family from jams and tricky crisis? Would you rather re-edit the example of their parents, so many years later?

Irritated, the top scriptwriter mutters and then shouts. That crap is for psychiatrists. Do you hear me?

She plays dumb and unblinking continues her storyline – Are you in the traditional role or you're looking for another inside, more suitable for the current situation? Do you want to be a rib with or without Adam? Always dancing cheek-to-cheek? Do you need well combined periods of society and solitude? With her phobias and the compulsion for the perfect finish of the necessary for tomorrow but made yesterday, is she as a money mint as she seems in public? Did she poetically distort the mom and dad royal couple? Did she idealized the father and built a thick wall against the true and possible love between a couple?

Dare to read without metaphors what really answered the expert after your long-winded speech. You're putting your foot in your mouth, you are too old for that nonsense and trick.

She insists not to disappoint Goldyale because she really needs a salary at all costs. While possible, she does not want to depend on anyone because when a father gives to a son, both laugh when a child has to give to a father, both cry. Why grief today with the sorrow of tomorrow. In one night and a lot of espresso, she assembles each shot with abundant dialogues, increases, removes and ties paying attention to the arches of dramatic tension to leave in suspense during the breaks for the five advertisements.

For the second session she goes ready and in slow motion she hands her work – Here are the diagrammed scenes for half an hour of transmission, as stated in your handbook of scripts, eureka , I hope he loves it.

It doesn't even take five minutes the review of her work. – Missus, again in your statement there no major conflict that allows or justifies one hundred twenty hours of interest for the viewer. Your work is very respectable and might be appealing for some snobs, but it lacks climax and antagonistic characters. Not a passionate rising line interrupted by obstacles, traps, jealousy, and external evil that allows us to stretch it. It is a comic tragedy, groups C and D. I recommend you in good faith to write giving advice to the lovelorn in those gossip magazines, there are many.

She doesn't even talk back. Parsimoniously she collects the papers. My dear friend, if this couplet as the wind wherever you want to hear it, you will be plural because felling claims it, when one carries friends in the soul...

In a language of perfect official fashion she says: – Listen, grandma, your writing is crap, but you are sappy after all. Would you rather record a theme for the noon revolutionary soap opera?

Is it by chance or her judge is of Spaniard descend that calls crap the unusable instead of old-fashioned. Anyway, that the specialist is right, who the hell cares for the contrived and abstract nonsense if an orphan needs a baby bottle or breast milk, if he wants to recover his crib or a pallet is enough, if he crawls and when walking requires walkers?

Perhaps it was penetrated by some poet of poets. Yeah right. Eugenio de Andrade and in Portuguese... You make a key, no matter how small, and enters into the house, you accept the sweetness, feels compassion for dreams and birds, evoke the heat, light, music in the corners, no you must say stone, you say window, do not be obscure, you say woman, child, stars ... There is a place ... where you lived and slept, at times, you're still alive.

One doesn't win or lose, go away or return, there is no far or near, nothing says good-bye or returns. One is still movable at the anchor.

6

SOMEBODY KEEPS TRACK of her, so what, who cares. Wandering is walking and walking searching for something similar to a homeland pulled out by the roots.

It has as much chance of triumphing as having a good marriage a single woman who brings triple dowry of old age, ugliness and poverty. She wanders with an eye on the superb mountain that is a compass but accepts with Chelique Sarabia... I do not know who I am... *They are the years maybe or the distress of being like a sailboat sailing randomly...* and she stumbles with posters that invite her – The City Hall invites you to the carnival festivities – You don't feel lonely, shriveled up and dilapidated, there is free party for young and old. Parade of floats and costume contest – Musical show from two to six at your Plaza Bolivar.

Oh, carnival, pure farce. The sovereign escorted by an entourage, King Momo with a scepter, a jester and courtesans. A theater of the senses in power, noise and laughter for four days. With Ash Wednesday you start the penance and admit the endless quarantine, apparent holy remedy.

In this time when everyone wants to be the other one, she does not use camouflage or amulets, she goes more denuded than ever of that umbrella without fabric that waters her under the slightest downpour. Return. Return – Pop, I want a queen costume, with a cap of sequins and beading – Talk to your mother, I don't have a clue. However, to go through the year I have to use different masks for each problem, ha ha ha.

Mom's dresser is a portmanteau of revelations. With her lipstick and pads for powdering her nose, that espionage challenge goes beyond the thresholds of the impossible and I am sure you don't know me.

The second fort, a tall oak armoire, grants amazing surprises to transgress a whole body. On the ladder she collates nylon stockings, a purse lined in precious stones, a whalebone fine lace corset, silver fox fur, a short belt with flexible grooves for a wasp waist and very long necklace of yellowed pearls. She is that another mother, the Miss and her father's fiancée, smiling and coquettish, waiting to get involved with a mazurka and other polonaise in between.

Requesting the permission of your majesty and power of mother and superior is a rough thing that she rehears in her mind and before the mirror but always fails acting on impulse – Mommy, I'm going to the masquerade – And where is that ruckus? – In the school – I am not so sure, it is a danger at your age-

At which not, yours? – How disrespectful, there must be your clown costume – Jeez, enough, it is ugly, it doesn't fit me anymore and the troupes now are of "negritas', mummies – There isn't another one, period- I want a Spanish dancer one, with hoop earrings, bracelets, chains, fans and everything – You're asking too much, before all was more modest, the Indians came dancing to awaken a snake and danced "la burriquita" and the children threw candies to the street from the windows without muddle and petition. That remains but it's not enough, and you haven't disguised yourself? What nonsense! Never. Have more important duties to perform. Besides, you know the world is mourning the Second World War and so much tragedy – life is serious –And Dad is not serious? He is kindhearted for little, unable to hurt anyone or touch the ground.

Definitely. Someone is following her, what will they take from her?

At five o'clock the mayor's musical show is at its peak. – here, here, shouts a legion of not so small kids that trample disguised as Pikachu, Teletubbies, Dragon Ball , but mostly they are like red berets dwarfs commanders, the "Chavecitos" in campaign to battle with an ammunition of water balloons and little confetti. Such struggle to be others, and are becoming more equal. Children's revolutionary carnival with a goal, indoctrinating almost from the cradle.

A commotion on the dance floor reveals distant echoes from the stage ... Caracas, the most beautiful, you are beautiful, the birthplace of the Liberator ... glorious lights with your wreath of hills around you ... Yes, the pasodoble, decorous tango and acid test to enter the party people club with moral that in the Argentine and public case dare to a ... I want to my heart to forget a crazy love ... but never a ... Smoking is a great, sensual pleasure, Smoking I wait for man I want ... because goodbye to furloughs and with punishment on the weekend. Hissing something similar to a slum milonga, swapping, getting wasted, is degenerate and to avoid problems ... I love so much my Caracas, its hill, its red roofs, its cute sky, the colorful flowers from Galipán ... Billo Frometa's waltzes I want to be maid of honor, of an elegant and attentive page in a royal court of some enchanted place. But with the next first beat claiming the old coachman ... Whoops! Isidoro, what a joke you played on me the day you went away you ... one puts the feet on the ground to fall where the stuff is, the Hotel Avila, columns and reception area of the colonial house , your first dance at fifteen, a bluish dress and four centimeters heels, with a visa to walk daubed. Crazy school trio, she with her gorgeous dress as pianist and singer, Carlitos on the accordion, Saul with the drums... Hey listen to my rhythm, good "pa'goza"... parents and guardians so ashamed of these wayward children, playing here cha-cha-cha, merengue, mambo and other gaudy beats as if this were a cabaret, El Pasapoga this and who knows what other in fashion, disreputable dancing place... C'mon rumbero, the rumba is about to start...

The uniformed ones sniff her trail undisguised. So what?

Today a raucous crowd overflows the square. She can barely distinguish on the stage the sound crew and what seems a flute, French horn, saxophone and tuba. The floor immerses her with frights by the appearance of a moving ta ta tan. *Oh, my uncle, oh, my uncle, at midnight drunk.... Oh Judge, I tell you the truth, carnival has come...,* merengues, wiggling and back pain. It seems that the group also plays trombone, clarinet, euphonium, oboe... *For that my soul is like the exquisite soul of the crystal, I love, cry, sing, dream...* End of the party?

Someone is kicking her, go figure.

An alert chill shivers her from heel to head recognizing, without having seen, the face of the boozer. – Your I.D., citizen – who are you, why are you chasing me, what do you want? Gee, the revolutionary police authority, from the behind you look like a kiddo – Mr. policeman, I am just passing by to see the carnival and I didn't bring any documents with me, but I live close by, if you want we can go to get it – Then don't drop off, shameless old bag, move it coz this thingamajig is over and the fuss ain't gonna last. Move it!

Although from the forties an up you don't wet the belly, taciturn, in flip-flops and Sunday gown, very short and bottle green, not realizing she had sunk into the cement couch on one side of the crowd and its debauchery, away from the warm tangle that stuns you go back to the square hooked to his hand – Daddy, those gentlemen who are on stage are they cops playing with drums as the tin soldier? – Something like that my little girl, it's an orchestra called martial because it plays marches, others say it is popular because it interprets pieces invented by the people, it is the same with the names -And I, why do I have two names? One for my mother, Alondra mistranslated, blessed be her memory – But the second is horrible, in my classroom all make fun- Well, tell them it's Brilliance. What's that daddy? – It means brightness because when you were born, you bring new light to us that we had no family in a country also new. The civil chief signed the first paper of your birth in San José and told us it was good to call you Fulgencia because it's a woman's name and is used here a lot. Your mom searched to find out and it's beautiful, it means the same as sunlight Happy? But you're a songbird.

She held her fury, she was afraid to respond the uniformed with a red cap, but when she sees him far from the barbed wire that protects the embankment, she

80

takes advantage he's tottering and does not carry his service firearm to spit loudly a primer of insults, yes, of the petty bourgeois she learned when she was a substitute in a nursery – and your mommy is as cute as a Georgia Peach? – Your mother wears thongs? – The cooch of your boo, if she has one. The extreme slut that bore you. And some of that repertoire, more refined.

It is great to feel this light; you explode while keeping the good manners. No man can serve two masters. But also you will have to thank infinitely   the hemlock, that municipal authority that broke her vigil because now she enjoys wide awake the nocturnal sound coming from the stand. It is and is not that of those Sundays at noon, on a square with a heroic statue, next to the cathedral and holding on to her father – Why do you force me to come with you? – My little girl, because you must learn not to be overwhelmed by the sounds of the jukebox, parties and radio that not always are music, then when you grow up, you'll seek your sound by yourself, the one that is more like you.

Now cadence flows more than that ringing in a strike of light and frothy vigor. A short-haired woman rules the roost. The group of performers is wearing ordinary clothes, and she even thought seeing some wearing a baseball cap – Dad, it's too hot, I want a lemon shaved ice, you didn't tell me why those musicians are dressed like that, as if we had snow here, with caps, jackets, buttons, and belts – Those kepis with visor are just a memory. Before the military encouraged their troop with uniforms and heavy artillery to go the ugly wars, but they realized that peace is better and more beautiful, so now they use musical instruments instead of weapons, do you understand?

She could never understand. From the news at the Rex cinema back in San Jose to the magazines of cable television, the ideal patriot quarters and liquidates exhibiting with natural or feigned elegance, a good cut wardrobe, casual or formal worthy of competing in the fashionable lofty catwalks groomed for genocide and hecatomb with an appearance and steps of triumphant touch.

It gets dark with a crescent moon, The Avila a greenish wall. A silence that surrounds it is about to sound. Little by little she livens up and arises the scrawling of the stage. Guitars and flugelhorn, bass and keyboard, at rest.

Suddenly a strange silhouette stands in the center and modulates *Summertime* with his trumpet, Aria, ballad, lullaby unfolds in a solo of enchantment. She, in the gloom, almost groping, goes forward looking to grab the figure that turns into flesh and beats the illusion. Entwining hers a strong and smooth hand. It's the deepest caressing on the bride and the doting mother, daughter and spouse, female and male, whore and respectable lady of Holy Spirit. For her, harbinger

82

of the shivering vertical pendulum, sole certainty, dance with no masks. For him, maybe another chance, just a tease, cutting a rug with a crazy old lady, but that's all, no way, lest the old square falls in love with me. My thing is family behind closed doors. No way!

Meanwhile, the sound and dream, their own murmur in swing dazzles them. No need of puppets or rocking chair. Oscillating skin to sin, with the fetal impulse of the most intimate concert. Jazz. Swing.

7

ALTHOUGH IT IS A HOLIDAY for the voting fair, she accelerates the daily grind. She fills the trash bins, sweeps and mops the floor from one end to the other, orders the receipts, sprays the walls with insecticide, and she even warns the residents about the rationed water. Never before that waterwheel seemed more obstinate, mostly useless. The steady rain of large and heavy dripping has turned muddy all her effort.

She admits that her bemoaning is unfair. Yes, she is confined to about forty meters, but she has a floor and a roof, the wanderer with bibles and scripts vanished. He, alas, Luis, finally love, and those in his gang, they are trustworthy friends. With the benefits, salary and tips she could buy this high-quality Christmas present, a small cassette player with headphones that she carries in the pocket of her neat apron or hanging around her neck.

Seven at night without moonlight. But... *the moon is not pale...* what this lady needs to be aroused... *oh, no, it's just his proximity...* he will come soon... And so, while she places the mended tablecloth used for special occasions, old poplin, embroidered in cross stitch, the voice of Nancy King sighs with... *It's not your sweet talk what gives me this feeling, oh no, it's only your closeness...* If he had come she would say – Listen love, without a melody it's the corniest bolero, and without lyrics another nice music, in intercourse of vocal knot it becomes almost perfection. And then he comments – Maybe the key of jazzing is that it manages to tense, without breaking, the ends of the tightrope between the common and the select... *When I'm in your arms and feel you so close, all my dreams come true...*

She is a genteel janitor. She sets two places with the decent china bought at a Christmas sale and does a duet with the delicious... *I don't need dim lights that intoxicate me...*polite way of asking him – Why the hell do you ask me to accompany you to the piano-bar or disco or clubs? I await for you here as long as necessary... *If you just allow me to always be by your side, the closeness of you...*

She agrees that The King is not a stellar diva but with ups and downs of some rack in her unbridled excitement, groans singing as she would do if she had that gift, before, during and after the encounter- Your proximity...is your favorite sung jazz piece, isn't it? – One of them, especially for you.

And it will be sonorous curtain of the anniversary dinner just for two, for nine months of love and postponed so many times that it now looks possible only in visions.

The studio apartment looks like she likes. It is the home of someone very sober, someone that was or might be a nun, said one morning the mother of a dweller who came to nose around. But no, sister of charity she will never be. All the stuff bothers her, that miscellany as much art as it would seem, museums exist for that. In a private complex the objects in excess portray its artifice, bewilder, weaken the senses and being together. And they last so much more than one does. Now junks that touch the memory and they are few. The Godmother in oil, with her sail boat, crag and the shore tree over gentle oil, but it is worth a whole lot of money, yes, yes, it is the gift of a Polish cousin who survived the family shipwreck in the forties and looks at the ocean with the eyes of a recently calved. Her sacred collection of little marionettes, varied in appearance, Louis' trumpet in its case, all the possessions of the same rank. Is that why shortly after that night of the criminal downpour countersigned by new laws of the revolution, when not even him, a messenger of the group could come, but yes the waters of the creek becoming a dirty stream, and she had to leave in a hurry from the cave about to be flooded and has been her home during the pregnancy to term, it was easy to gather her precious objects in a small suitcase.

Certificates of birth, marriage and divorce, high-school, bachelor with masters to be perfect in this and beyond, a bunch of documents and certificates with a fresh stamp of aunts, children, siblings, stamped paper, tracing paper, legal size and pentagram, lined, newspaper, desiccant, charcoal, white, an arsenal of papyrus to barely survive in her country so that same day she decided to change her given name and the certificates starting with the birth one.

Black time of much and rotten breath, of the water that shall just flow, broken evening. Noah, women at five thousand years of time. Rescue of her uncertain tomorrow although mandatory by couples in your salvation ark. Then, there you have her facing you at hand, ramshackle blue Bible with its threadbare and sole left cover, as old as your elders. And he, his Quixote Sancho in one body of letters. I hesitate because The Little Prince that I always imagine for the famous deserted island, but of course, at least with an Antoine Saint-Exupery, in person, to share such lonely beauty – Where are you from Antoine? – *Where am I from? From my childhood as from a country – Stories, music, movies, cartoons? – Yes, childhood, that great territory we all come from…*

But it is final, at the right moment, when nobody comes, that it is better to be accompanied by our every day pair, the sane and the insane, which make survival clearer.

And at the minute of choosing the pair of voices for relief at the wrong time, it was you Louis, with the jovial weight of your hundred years, with your strong black arm and who rescued me from the raging water. I heard that booming voice in San Jose, attached to the window bars where I was doing homework. It was coming from the RCA Victor apparatus to lighten the daily ordeal, the circulatory system, the square root, the list of insects, a bunch of caciques, boredom. Listening to ... *What a wonderful world* ... rough tenderness inside and around, it was one loud and fun play, sparkle and sweetness, full-throated and blow in metal tone.

Tonight does not sound his magic trumpet, it was his-your ugly, hoarse voice, but so Armstrong, so my father, it turned me into a protected child, at last. To match he approached the prodigy of very high notes and deep lows, cascading, that Sarah Vaughan dedicated to me in that same tone of Trinita, very fat, black and thick lips, always ready to put to sleep the little angels of the missus and the mister., foreigners that will be over there, until very late in the clothing business.

The photographs album is very heavy. She takes the first one, in sepia of her paternal great-grandfather, cantor of liturgies, and the most recent, in Technicolor, granddaughter that sounds divine, a rumor of secure spring.

Which of her marionettes will she be allowed to take? They all fit into a cellophane bag.

With those belongings in the small red plastic suit-case, circumventing wells and streams that as a rosary emerge from the steep street while her block and building neighbors flee in droves stuffing their cars and shouting – Don't forget the refrigerator – the TV fits here – Don't you leaving the dominoes tables – Bring well-filled crates – You have to find a place for the microwave oven.

They have the security of a portion of wet and treach-erous soil, but theirs, and the experience that they are not from the slums, bridge or the hills, that their credit and installment purchases come from wages and some commission under the table to make ends meet. They are the hindrance that nobody has or pities, in the middle of everything and nothing, they never reach the category of redneck, marginal or bootleg or destitute, a species that copes with beer, soda and a fat burger. A class of dispensable discomfort for those of arepa without cheese, and the caviar ones.

The classless Missus flees without looking back. She's still wearing her topaz taffeta gown, with flounces and lace. A silk tie crowns her bangs hair-style. There is a reason that gown resisted decades, waiting for its second destination. Also the satin shoes, elongated tip and stilettos, they were intact, very outmoded and comfy. They say that one should adorn oneself for the predicament. Tonight was her revival of quasi-official girlfriend. When Clark Gable saved Vivian Leigh lifting her in his powerful arms so the wind of war wouldn't take her, the beautiful gown she wore, didn't get wrinkled, or burned, or wet, it was impeccable while coming down the endless spiral staircase.

She then leaves with her only treasure, bunch of papers and those relics that sooner or later, will also be dust.

If I had time I would go back to take out of the ten, at least two films on videotape, Chaplin rescuing himself from the snow storm in The Gold Rush and the tough Bogart in his rebellious Casablanca giving in to the tenderness of... *As time goes by*... beseeching the pianist Sam... *Play it*... Play... *Play that again*... to revive the scene of years ago in Paris when Ingrid Bergman tells him – *The Gestapo seized the city, the world crumbles and we fall in love – Yes, inopportunely, where were you ten years ago*? and it was when she realized she had deeply in and sewn the one of The Postman, that Mario Skarmeta who with Burning Patience embodied for Neruda, in the big screen and from a rustic microphone, the sound of the tiny waves and the surge, the winds of the cliff and through the bushes, the bells of the church of Our Lady of Pain in the Italian beach and the heart beat of his unborn child. Because it is true that one must be attentive to sounds and also that poetry, like God and love can only exist in the imagination of those that need them.

White water, blessed be, ready to quench that night would never be of idyll, she needs her jazz in the background, because listening to it, you would say, is like every first time, full of challenges and amazement, never routine. But in such a different occasion, I say, it should be placed in the inner table, and undoubtedly also in bed, some sign of the past. And nothing better than water in the maternal fine glass jar, container of the ancient and eternal family that has resisted, alas, all changes of the wandering cycle. Delight is the most pure water to moisten the delicacies she prepared before the damn deluge believing that even under a flood of rocks and logs El Zorro, Superman would come, he.

But suddenly the racket of a great silence. It was when she paid much attention to the noise. The ravine bordering the avenue, a trickle of silent urine spiraling down from her beloved beautiful and traitor mound, bed and waste in waters, the sea becomes rough and roars. Her ear senses the liquid avalanche, only then she initiates the escape and leaves the janitor's studio carrying all her wealth in a suitcase in tow. Picking up the pace, she goes on without the Phantom, she runs, he will not come, nor your sailorman Popeye, not even the Chapulin Colorado, beat it, you're risking your life with that childishness.

Louis sings hoarse a luminous ballad that opens with the verse I saw you standing in the sun ... and goes on

... There is nothing within me but dreams ... seeing you there, under the sun, I said to myself, you are to me ... And then, this time he culminates in a radiant trumpet solo ripping walls, stones and heaven itself, without a single blemish.

After the downpour, taking refuge in the shelter of the pariahs and feeling as a fish out of the water, as she dreamed she was the Sleeping Beauty, she was given back the broken suitcase with all her stuff but without a single paper. When the courses went back on their track, under the drizzle, she turned on her portable luxury of luxuries and she could hear a thousand times that carnal and blessed psalm, eternal cadence adds and multiplies for perennial vacuum that divides and subtracts. And she began this chaotic draft of the lady who never gave up because she wrote.

Where could you be Luisito? You don't come or look for me. Why don't you show up Luis? The day before yesterday, when leaving the house in the rainy morning, you say I'll back early and mention a contract at some beach casino ... Macuto? Oh my Macuto ... the square where I was a traveling pigeon, happy fiancée for the imagined honeymoon in the palatial hotel overlooking the sea, jumping on the beach grapes boardwalk, to be immersed in the seaside pleasure, Las Quince Letras counted once and again, because they are fifteen letters, for one to start the vice for words, where a handsome, dark-skinned lifesaver that grew old and departed, he was my real Prince Valiant, relieving that little girl's panic of the sea and healing apprentice scratches. Lucho dear, you go away and get lost, you go and separate. It looks like you disappeared into thin air, perhaps swallowed by a river, maybe by the sea.

Here, where they demand revolutionary peace, identity and courage to normalize all, our meeting turned into murky water, your proximity disappeared, but there goes on and on sweet flowing of singing, while I weep this coward chronicle about a stubborn drizzle. The ones that impregnates the outside and drowns the inside. Searching for the echo of how many souls? bloomed in the ash that mercilessly erased their voices and the narrow coastline.

THEY AND JUST IN ELEVEN MONTHS

1

FELLOW CITIZEN: WITH THIS CATACLYSM in Vargas I'm out of contact and I haven't been able to get hold of you for two days. My cell phones lines and the office ones are crossed or not working. I feel obliged to submitting you this confidential letter in your hands; I hope you can decipher my handwriting. I ratify what I told you on Thursday after the meeting. We managed to dismantle the anti-revolutionary cell run by some guy named Luis. Surnamed Umbra, alias The Rooster. I'm told that this leader and part of the subversion are undocumented, the detention was in flagrante at the janitor's studio in the condo we had been watching for a couple of months, If this melodrama of La Guaira allows it, tomorrow I'll inform you in person about the background and to carry out the attack against high officials, of course, no one against you,

There is a mess in our files because the tragedy of the missing and those who lost their documentation makes masses of people seek and renew their identification card which slows us to know the identity of this faction. There were difficulties from the beginning because they are poising as a musical group, they seized a deposit of flutes, marimbas, batteries and other supplies in armored linings that they tell me were intermingled with automatic weapons, orchestral right wing so to speak. It has to be checked well.

At the moment of the raid, the clan leader, a chunky element with afro hair was cleaning a trumpet as heavy as submachine gun and he resisted our agents with the story of an unlawful entry. The dude says he is from the La Guaira coast, for years he was a truck driver of the vegetables market to the capital. But it's there, with all the ruins, where we'll confront him.

…Farmer, farmer, oh-dark-hundred…And you have to get up because work calls. And it has to be early, to sell your crop. Hey landlady, say what you sell, Farmer, say what you sell…

Okay, we're about to corner the alleged owner of the apartment they used as hideout, and who served as janitor. She is known in the organization of the counter-revolution as Fulgosa and they assure me she has a criminal record for her misconduct. For now, in this country we do not know who is who and who was or who will be who, everyone can be someone or several or no one, total quagmire.

I attach the newsletter prepared for the media because speaking at the rally about an assassination about to happen, they are speculating on whether it is a pre-election trick to focus attention. Send it back to me with the carrier and with your approval, is extremely urgent because the international attention is here at the mudslide disaster. The yokel Luis is already at the headquarters of La Guaira to confront him with his people. Tear this message up.

...He goes out with his load, overjoyed for the city, oh, the city. He carries in his mind a world full of happiness, oh, happiness. He's thinking about remedying the situation, of the home that is his dream... And happy goes the *jibarito* singing and saying along the way, if I sell all my load, my dear God, a suit for my mum I'm going to buy...The whole morning goes by and no one comes to buy his load. Everything, everything is deserted; the people are in need, oh, in need... That lament is heard everywhere.

2

HELLO COMRADE, I'm XR, I'm calling from the Division and it pisses me off that you don't answer the phone, I'm leaving a voicemail and note down. Tell the older brother that as for now we know little about the bitch, biddy, no known trade, a street-walker who previously lived in a single and overnight she got a gig in the building where we caught the small group that was plotting. Tell him that in the Division they are reviewing several cases of a swindler which they say is called Fulgencia but she impersonates different people changing clothes and identity cards, she's requested for her misdeeds, yadda, yadda, yadda, but we have to catch her in flagrante delicto, and take her to a control prosecutor. About him, tell him he's lecherous, here in what is left of the jail he is arrogant; he used to lurk in the streets as ready for partying. You tell he calls himself Luis Mendez. With so many wet dead bodies he just whistles and whistles and fiddles and clatters as having a bongo all day and he is here as partying, sings and sings without stopping, but there is no way to make him blow the whistle on his buddies or the gats.

…I'mma happy, I don't know what I feel, I am singing like the river, like the wind, like the hummingbird that kisses the flower in the morning, like a mocking-bird leaving its song in the savannah…

Hey, these fucking guys always colluding and they don't wear hoods but they are street-savvy, this one beguiles with his face. Now he swears that the thug is another one, that for many years they have confused him with someone else, he likes partying, that's why they call him Luis Grillo, he never throws a stick when working and every once in a while and in hiding. He says he is a dude that plays the trumpet and commands the members but in dances and rumbas here, and in the country, when they are doing it they don' even smell liquor. He says music is more than his woman, just partying .Without an I.D. we can't confront anyone and without the Law of Slackers and Criminals, you know, we cannot keep him in the hoosegow because we'll hear from the Civil Chief, the Prefect and the others. Tell the boss that we will have a fit because the staff of our facilities doesn't appear, many are from Caraballeda, Carmen de Uria and around. Give me instructions to leave him here caged and see what we can so that the stoners don't bit the shit out of him, we can't gamble everything and lose, over comrade.

…He is out, Julian Pacheco is out of the hell in which he lived, amulets or witchcraft were of no avail They took his hallacas, his guitar and maracas, they left him without his tails but the poor man is out …He's back, it is true that he came looking ugly but full of joy, to sing to his girls, his boleros and guarachas and tell Caracas, that Julian is back ... They tell me he's skinny but happy and rascally, they tell me that he is bald and his pigtail dropped. But the truth gentlemen, is that the drums are sounding saying to the dancers that Pacheco is out ... Let's all party....

3

DEAR LISTENERS, Notiradio interrupts its regular programming for breaking news.

They are denouncing before the People's Defense Court sexual harassment against the victims.

This aberration took place in several shelters, with intimidation and not stopping before those present, or the age of the injured ranging from twelve years old girls to venerable grandmothers. The violations were committed by drunken officers wearing uniforms and armed to the teeth in the immediate days following the landslide.

…But when I see a "caraqueña", I get excited, when I see a "caraqueña", then I do go crazy… There are no girls as the ones from La Pastora, no, no, no, there are no chickens as the ones from La Florida, no, no, no, there are no faces as the ones from San Jose, no, there are no girls as the ones from Las Mercedes, no, no…

The complainants prefer to remain anonymous for fear of reprisals against their physical integrity and that of their families. With signatures recorded they request the immediate investigation of the outrage they did to that portion of women, some already well into the senectitude. They refer the case of one victim who suffered a severe nervous breakdown and had to be taken by a municipal ambulance to an ambulatory medical post set up in one of the city airports. The old woman, in her forties, whose first name is unknown but recognized by several of those present as the hugely popular Saint Fulgia, who sells catechisms and other religious books dressed as a secular nun and preaches as an evangelical. Sometimes, say others, she swaps any existing odds and ends but holy cards, almost always bible, nothing else, although some declarant said that she even offers animals lottery, play three and lotto, she tell stories and sings in the jeepney in exchange for a few cents.

In her wanderings she often rides the metro bus, but mostly she goes on foot, door-to-door along the urban geography, especially on the busiest streets of the metropolis and its surrounding areas. People believe that she already had a steady job because they hadn't seen her for months in the selling hustle, but with the great downpour she reappeared as a victim of said abuse.

...I'm selling a closet, four chairs and a cage, a hardly used portable gas stove and a set of dominoes, the cot I don't sell because I sleep in it, the cot I don't sell because I sleep in it...

4

COLLEAGUE: I'M BACK at the headquarters of the Directorate but with the lousy phones and interlinked, I rather use this mean again to convey in writing grade thirty three orders from the higher authorities that force requesting your fast intervention on the alleged violation of Human Rights in Vargas.

It leaked into the press a host of comments regarding it. Specifically, it is going to be denounced, at any moment, by the large national newspapers, the disappearance of a certain Luis whose last name may be Douglas taken and shoved from his house by a shock squads, before his wife, and neighbors, pushed into a station wagon with the acronym of a state security agency.

...Gotsa be careful in the slum, gotsa be careful on the sidewalk, gotsa be careful anywhere, they are looking for you, for your bad habit...

The bereaved have toured hospitals, morgues and other places, without locating his whereabouts. The individual left or was taken from here to the coast, it may even be the same conspirator I notified you about yesterday. There is not even the slightest trace of his trajectory since he was apprehended, which can be proven with all the photographs taken at the moment of being caught, and already widely circulating for publication. Perhaps he is the subject in question.

Antisocial guy, described as tall, crinkly hair, heavy built, slanted eyes, about thirty years old, renowned robber from Catia La Mar, an expert on mugging and emptying shops and houses in Caracas, and now he might have returned to loot the vacated villas and residences close to his neighborhood sunk in the mud. His war nickname is Lucho and he's protected by his gang because he is a party animal, he loves a soiree with harp and maraca players to distribute food and booze, in the slum he is a show off, he says he's a musician by profession. It is said that he spends a lot of time in Blandin, but his refuge is there with his local cohort. Who leaves no trace is his wife, they say that sometimes janitor, but very likely she is the retailer selling seditious material undercover as prayer books.

It's imperative to immediately respond to this fact not only to clarify the ongoing schemed plan but by the local and global impact that may mean. Everyone's eyes are on us for the terrible events of Vargas, and such a problem with that guy Luis may lead to an internal and external catastrophe worse for us than the natural disaster occurred. I'm expecting your report. Burn this paper.

...I'm goin' to town, today is my day, I will brighten all my soul... As much as I work and I can never go to the blowout... I'm goin' to town to gulp down a gallon, and when I return there will be no more coal... The field is beautiful, but to town I'm goin' to cut a rug. If you don't come, better this way, because I don't know what will become of me...

5

REGARDING the missing due to the tragedy, among the reports reaching our briefing room, almost at the closing of this edition printed at midnight, we report about the corpse of a man, mulatto, about forty years old, robust, one meter seventy, wearing jeans, stripped t-shirt and barefoot, that appeared yesterday in the margins of the Guaire, via Pablo VI of Petare Neighborhood, presenting three gunshots in the back of his neck, and recorded a time of death of about four days. It is presumed he was killed in cold blood somewhere else and then abandoned there. Young residents bike riding alerted about the finding.

...I blow you away, Mr. Casimiro, what I go after, I get, what sharpshooting, goodness gracious, buddy, you can't avoid the bullet. Pay me the *fuerte* that I lent you, six months ago, counting last month... If you don't pay me Mr. Casimiro, I swear I'll blow you away. Casi, casi, Casimiro...

There came to the location site Homicide, Ocular Inspection and Legal Medicine commissions. Firefighters from the East rescued the remains. One of them told this reporter that despite the relative decomposition that erased the factions, looking at him, he seemed to remember those of a wonderful flautist or saxophonist of the municipal bands featured outdoors on weekends and holidays, and who has always looked as a twin or has an extraordinary similarity to Luisito Dos, the dreaded scourge of the slum, a girl's rapist who avoided being lynched by a group of dwellers weeks ago and whose photograph frequently appeared in the crime reports. It's speculated that the body, like so many others in these dark days, can come from the coast and fell into the Catuche ravine which high water level dragged him to the river running through the city. It is expected the activation of the fingerprints, and if necessary, the study of the dental records, once the situation of the policy labs is resolved to resume their work, suspended because some of their premises were flooded.

...The other night I went by the corner of Las Gradillas, I had a nightmare that I almost screamed. They pulled me by the feet, grabbed me by the hands and brother you cannot imagine the shock that I took... In the corner of Las Gradillas there appears a ghost, with the wooden leg and face of an old man... Although you may not believe it, there appears a ghost, if you don't believe it, ask Ruperto...

6

WE YIELD THIS SPACE of Notitele, channel 8, to present a brief special report prepared by our department of events.

Children call her by the alias Grandma Ful because she is always full of candy, a child told his father, and through that lead we got to know the existence of a virtual network of senior prostitutes using infants to make bigger the drug trade and other illicit activities.

As if she were one of many seniors wanting to sunbathe, the woman usually goes to the playgrounds in the early hours of the day. But they say that she especially likes to swing for hours. Her innocent facade seems to conceal one of the alleged keys of the chemicals and psychotropic substances trade, and she has a history of conspiracy with her buddy nicknamed Luis. Both in the slums as in selected and middle-class neighborhoods.

It is assumed that her modus operandi is to collect dozens of children ten and older trained in all levels as tipsters, vendors, caregivers and even what they call robots, aimed at physically eliminating the enemies of rival gangs and those in the police sector that confiscate the product.

She is believed to come from a nice family for her professional way of communicating, persuading and seducing the little ones with her looks almost always maternal. Her way of dealing with narcotics would be through games, as if she were a child swapping candies, toys and cartoons for marijuana cigarettes, LSD papers, pills of a drug known as Ecstasy, crack rocks, powders of pure cocaine and basuco. It is another right wing quisling.

It is rumored that the mechanism was discovered by comments from some preschoolers and custodians of the parks that the suspect frequents, both have contributed to preparing a police-artist's sketch. She looks like a clown, it may even be a male disguised, maybe a travestite, says one of the guards. As she is kind of short and skinny she perches on all the equipments in the playground mostly on the swings, and blends in with the little dudes, suggests another one.

Meanwhile, members of the detachments of the national military plan surmise that there may be complicity and the confusing maneuver by some involved. The only police who patrol these wastelands are those who are going to collect the permission given to them by the bandits of the drug, of all ages, to operate on the perimeter of what they call their place, in full freedom, say spokesmen of the sentry box. And when they appear, stoned or drunk till they drop, it may take days, even weeks and they never report to their superiors, murders, thefts or accidents. See what they see and hear what they hear, they are blind and deaf. But they are posing as whistleblowers to mislead. It would be better not to stick out around here, conclude the informants.

Although there aren't yet images on our channel, we have advanced the information because news to be confirmed report that several days ago the notorious woman and part of her group were cornered, and as they resisted, there was a shooting that apparently took them down. We will be on the lookout for any new developments or confirmation issued by the police agency.

Life is full of surprises... and Pedro Navaja fell on the sidewalk... And believe me people, although there was noise, no one came out, there weren't any curious. No questions, no one wept. Only a drunk tripped with the two bodies. He took the gun, the dagger, the pesos and left. And tripping him left singing outta tune, the chorus that here I brought you and is the message of my song... Life is full of surprises...

7

MR. OFFICE DEPUTY DIRECTOR: I'm sending you the requested material that I hastily drafted with the limited data we have in this office because of the chaos due to the storm along the coast.

They nicknamed him Luis. Houses and banks mugger, he is said to lead a host of goons and light-fingered friends with sticky fingers. He was arrested driving a Ford vehicle sought by the Antimano Police Station when the patrol ordered him to stop he launched a grenade that didn't explode. After a heavy exchange of gunfire he died in Catia Hospital from where he was sent to be examined by the forensic and ballistics experts.

Put your hand in your pocket, pull out and open your knife, be careful. Keep your ear on the ground; many big shots have been killed... Moon Street, Sun Street...

In addition to the device and a GL nine-millimeter pistol, they seized maracas, a *cuatro*, a microphone and a bathing suit so they assume he was returning from a bacchanal on the beach and disturbed by an overdose of alcohol or drugs.

Commissioner Sinforoso Arcay gave confusing details about the individual. Participant in crimes committed with his cronies known as The Party Loving for liking to liven up any party they go and they ask to be paid with Guarapita, a Cuba Libre and rum. They are accused of planning the escape of a prisoner who, with the complicity of a relative escaped the La Planta Jail following the rainfall in La Guaira and was detained for an alleged attack on personalities of the revolutionary government.

Although all the identification services are in hiatus or working at half-throttle, and the fingerprinting service is not working, it was reported his name was Luis and was carrying false documentation with a license in theory, musical theory and composition techniques, and as owner of the stolen car which he was driving wearing a mechanics overall and is going through expertise.

The street is a concrete jungle with wild animals, of course... There is no one out overjoyed, wherever expect the wors... Juanito Alimana with viciousness reaches the desk... People are afraid of him, beware of him, to collar him one has to be a brave, and although stole everyone's money, everyone comments, nobody denounces him.. If they put him behind bars, the next day he's out because a cousin, is in the police force...

8

SURFER: THIS E-MAIL is urgent. We know that Internet and newspapers don't reach the slums, but we
can try, read it and circulate it because we all have a
mother, and luckily some of us will leave this place in
the same boat. This is a word of mouth review, but
directly from me, because the newspapers didn't report any behind the scenes of the old folks' demon-
stration yesterday, and I saw it. They toured several
government agencies, Capitol, Social Security, Min-
istry of Finances and Miraflores Palace, no repre-
sentative, director of President of the new republic
spoke to them.

The pilgrims in peaceful pilgrimage were asking, as
always the homologation of their pensions and retirement payments with the official minimum wage because the allowance they get dissolves like salt in the
water due to inflation, and they can hardly afford a
lousy daily meal.

Downtown was paralyzed by traffic congestion. I left
the car parked on the street and I could see with my
own eyes, hear with these ears, the via crucis of the
retired workers, almost in rags, how their demonstra-
tion was broken up first by the tear gas coming from

a riot a few blocks away, because there was also another union protest and another of the ruling party. Suddenly, magically, armed masked men emerge in hordes, infiltrating the elderly and shouting at them to leave because they are undermining their legitimate march, theirs, who are workers really revolutionary as they seek to claim wages and salaries, and not like them, the little old people, who are beggars, living on waste, as assholes.

…How much work is finding a job, what to do. How much work it is not to work… As if she lacked everything in life, Concepcion looks up to the sky. As if the world was falling on her, Concepcion told her grief…

She faced them as spokeswoman, a very petite, older, middle-aged little woman, still in shape; she looked as a matriarch holding a bible, protesting the outrage saying that she was a social activist in factories and unions since before they were born. The team of the ruling party member screaming shut the hell up, enemy, mercenary, wrinkled raisin, smooth out with starch, wash the cobwebs off, you gotta go to the nursing home, you stink, and other improprieties. And when she answered her voice was lost in the ruckus, that racket and shots in the air.

At the arrival of the patrol car with its squad, she slipped away and they handcuffed a disable man crawling with two crutches while the other fellows, with gray hair, were repressed with threats and more than one smack. I asked a policeman why they took those unfortunates without even questioning them. He said the old bigmouth carrying the book had just escaped again in the face of his armed colleagues, she is a famous stirrer, who attacks the government pretending to be a huckster and assistant in buses and is being closed in with an order to apprehend her. Just like that.

Use this compass pilot, and look at yourself in that mirror, If you aren't a supporter of the new government, prepare your raft, because they don't' even respect their own mother. Make a chain and globalize this fear.

...With an old woman I don't wanna be, allergic to wrinkles I am, with an old woman I don't wanna be without the dentures she won't kiss me. Listen to what I tell you, not even if she has a new car, or a lot of dough, no way in hell, I'd rather go to... work...

9

HELLO COMRADE, I'M XR and I'm calling back because it is urgent, prick up your ears, I'm at a pay-phone, do not ask, write down and give it to the doctor. It turns out that that snake is the chief and she is in charge. An old bag is worth a lot, I was told she did all kind of businesses, she sold stuff and marijuana and catechism books, but now it seems she's the owner of Fulgida Moon, do you remember, the big house there in the Baralt that outside is shabby and just for blabbering and getting smashed, but upstairs one cuts loose with those cute chicks ha ha. Well, that is supposed to be a bunker for ammunitions. Someone came to dish the dirt on that.

A buddy assures me that is busty, sings couple and she gets into fondling, cockteaser, because she is an old square you know. She takes care of the cash register, she's called many names and her friends know her as the Sexygenarian, money –grabber, oligarch because as they say, stingy, that's why she doesn't like this revolution but she gets into a ruckus against it.

Right now her right hand is another Judas like her, reactionary half-breed, petulant, they call him Luigi, but he must be Luis, the traitor to the fatherland, by the way dude, you haven't told where he is. One is going on and on and on and nothing, no one tells me what is going on.

Stop dead in you tracks, bro. I'm drinking some booze to chill out and warm up, and on the TV in the bar they are showing a photo of the wanted since the day before yesterday, and the other guy here tells me, shit, Mama Fu is fucked up, and then I take out from the pocket the torn photocopy of the photography that you gave me in the office, and I think it's the same face of Fulgencia, or whatever her name is, or they are twins, but she is such a common face that maybe is just my imagination and she isn't the same bitch. Watch out in El Poliedro and the barracks where there are the damaged, to see if the codger, the mad as a hatter that plays the trombone and his charanga, either they were saved or drowned, damn it. I have to find out what happened with the muso after we put him in the hoosegow, and whether she is or not the chick.

Answer and stand in for me pal, with this trap and afeared for my sister and nephews that live in my house in Maiquetia, and the rain that doesn't stop, so much tall tale, that there are four thousand, forty thousand dead, everyone has their own axe to grind.

…We are robbers of the Baralt, look out, the streets ain't safe. Yesterday we mugged one, we took his gun, if he comes back for it, we ain't giving it back…

If we hadn't ought come, we hadn't be bagged and they warn ya, now we're in the hoosegow...

10

MR. FIRST PROSECUTOR: In response to your request I send you a dossier with some of the steps taken so far to uncover the plot against our process by a small group that masquerades as revolutionary and liberal anti-system.

Fourteen witnesses, some reliable, others questionable, have declaimed before the Fourth Prosecutor of Intelligence of the Counterespionage Service that a month ago began the investigation about the false undercover insurgent. All informants are guaranteed discretion. I attached some basic samples.

...Officer Eustoquio Rondon Fraiz reported that the accused confronted him with a knife when he tried to detain her for being undocumented. It was during one of the last carnival shows, she was disguised as a menial he said, and she seemed to be drunk because since he began to follow her until the confrontation, she staggered as if she were sleepy, she hummed phrases, challenged him, insulted him with expletives and doused his eyes with a liquid dye containing confetti so he was unable to tie her hands and take her to the nearest police station. When he returned with motorcyclists she had disappeared from the place...

…An ex-soldier, Narciso Urquía Trejo, suspected of belonging to an urban commando who also works for the border counter-guerrilla, arrested for deserting during the events of Vargas, acknowledged that he maintained an intimate and short relationship with the woman when he arrived at the quarters where he was guarding the rain refugees. It was consensual and not rape as announced by the press, and she warned him she had concubines...

...Corporal Pedro Ermenegildo Rodulfo Pérez who was on his day off and went to a mall recently opened in Chacao, turned to the commission of inquiry to confirm what motivated him to follow her, the only time he saw her were her legs, because she wore shorts and being her clothing clearly very worn out, he declared, she was leaving the store with what looked like a very large and very heavy box that made her difficult to walk, and therefore he believed that she seemed like someone that had robbed a business and that there were other criminals in a car parked somewhere waiting for her. He ceased the investigation at the crowded subway car where she got in, and because he needed to do some family errands on that day...

…Very important is the statement of an illegal entrepreneur, Oto Rodales, from the textile industry, whose identity is still in doubt and under investigation for being a transient and expired documents, who appeared to collaborate as a volunteer, he said, terrified by the criminal wave of violence plaguing the country after the flood. He said seeing the photo of the woman whose arrest warrant was disseminated in all media, recalled that she was one of his employees as a seller of biblical texts and deliverer of samplers but proved to be a high-school graduate or a doctor, a radical left wing oratory but a traitor to the cause, who reminded him that of the continental armed struggle in his college years in the sixties, thus, he decided to dispense with her services because he is not a politician. It caught his attention the rancor of her clichés sentences against imperialism, capitalism and private property but what made him more suspicion was that she tries to look very mystical too, preacher and huckster about talks her ears off on the topic and she does not let anyone to lip off. He also warned that she is very aggressive and has obscene attitudes and gestures; she even dances flamenco and does striptease...

Mr. Prosecutor: Our investigation is well directed, it is increasing the number of those who want to testify to catch this dangerous spy, with extreme ability to camouflage and who seems to be a cornerstone of an ultra antigovernment team with a well supported structure in regards to tactics and strategies of the right.

…What nosey people, what nosey people, what nosey people, commie, they ain't given nuttin'. If I wear patched trousers and shirt, they say that what happens is that I have almost all my money in a barrel, what nosey people, commie …

11

GOOD MORNING audience of World Noticable.

A cameraman from the Transglobo agency recorded the possible reappearance of Fulgoria Follkowitz, international terrorist form past decades.

The video shows fairly lured commissions because the shots were made on the fly, amid difficult tasks of cooperation and rescue of victims of the storm that hit northern Venezuela a week ago. The images were captured at an improvised heliport around Caracas.

Some will remember the famous anarchist born in a Polish village or in a South American village; it was never a clear version of her origin, and in the course of her thirties wandering years she managed to acquire several nationalities. Fugitive always, as if the planet were hers, she could circumvent the persecutions for her extraordinary ability to escape the traps that she was tended to judge her, thus, he was given the nickname Lizard. Easily blending, she suddenly vanished from the world stage and was considered dead or possibly hidden in a country in Africa or Asia, although for her character of ideological sign, for her violent activism 'of protest and dissent without defined political ideology, it it's not known which regime could have protected her.

The French, camera operator Piere Anio, veteran in this journalistic source during the Cold War, explains he found her, almost certainly, discovering her Chameleon face already somewhat senile, as she was also nicknamed, in a woman that hugged rag dolls, waiting with a group of survivors in the stricken Latin American nation. He refocused and almost suffered a shock from the impression.

He lost sight of her in the few minutes he needed to replace a roll of film for his movie camera as his equipment was flooded in the swamp. When requesting her whereabouts to the guardians of the place, amid a chaos of Revelation by the emergency, they replied that group of females and children were sent in a helicopter, course unknown, perhaps to the capital, for the time being.

Different governments dispatched requests to expedite the search and verify if in fact she is the legendary figure who was accused of starring in a string of bombings and sabotage in various parts of the world. Anio reports that the last picture filed in Paris, you have it on the screen, is from sixteen years ago when they surprised the fugitive hidden under the habits of a nun during a papal address to a group of pilgrims who were listening to him outside on the square of St. Peter's Basilica.

We will pass on to you any new developments we get.

...Everybody returns to the land where they were born, to the incomparable spell of its sun, everybody returns to the corner from which they skedaddled, where perhaps more than a love flourished. When the last lone tree, how many times we dream, everybody returns on the memory lane, only the time of love will never return...

12

WHEN THE DIRECTOR of the Sunday weekly newspaper asked me for a article on the news that struck me most so far this month, as a daily reporter of events did not hesitate on selecting what at first sight is one of many and may go unnoticed by common but that managed to get me out of this drafting table and return to street work long as three years ago as intern in this newspaper.

The initial bulletin states that eight women were injured when a bus covering the Llanito-Silencio urban route was held up. A couple of juveniles boarded the bus and while one of them aimed at the driver, the other ordered that all men get off and stripped from the women watches, earrings and purses. Then he took out of his koala a butcher knife, short and sharp knife, with which he scratched hands, feet and faces of the passengers, insulting them with obscenities while wounding them. He mercilessly and violently attacked the oldest of all; Fulita a peddler very much liked in those vehicles where she tries to make a living every day, against all odds, sometimes as collector but almost always selling prayer booklets and trifles.

After they went mobbing for an hour, they left the unit in La India traffic circle at the end of Avenue Paez of El Paraiso, where they left the driver tied and with a gag.

The complaint specifies that the more furiously attacked was taken to Magallanes Hospital where she remains in the intensive care since the wounds are of the utmost gravity. The witnesses, bruised and full of indignation are regular users of this transport and report that due to the flood in December Mrs. Fulgita lost her job as doorwoman in a residence and her life partner disappeared, and she been trying to make some money in sales, as a storyteller who entertains the passengers with her good humor. She is tireless, they say, she rests only on the Sabbath. She speaks really cool, they add, as she is a teacher, she tells the tales backwards but spicing them up, sometimes one doesn't understand everything but still, one dies laughing. She always carries a tape recorder so we can listen to songs and verses in other languages that she repeats singing in Spanish, because she said very naughtily, that she had a love affair with an Englishman, a Jew, a Portuguese and an Italian and therefore thoroughly recognizes those languages, from a great and rich source.

And they do not just understand the savagery of the miscreant against this old lady, straight hair with yel-

lowish straw tufts, who usually creates acts as a co-
median, as well as counting the change, sometimes
sings, recites, dances and stomps her feet on the bus
corridor livening up the trip as if it were a rolling
show. Insist the witnesses – You see, it is very sad
because she would advise us, hear my audience, for
the sake of the flowers one must also irrigate the
thorns and she always ended the stories saying –
Count on me.

They conclude the story explaining that at the precise
moment when she tried to stroke the aggressor's head
and with endearment wanted to convince him, to at-
tenuate his anger, she approached the boy saying that
they were just kids, and who teaches a child is like
creating him again healthy and she offered to tell him
a nice story, at that moment, he responded with more
anger and stabbed her.

The gang of robbers wore clothes and footwear of
known brands, sports caps with slogans, dark, elongated sunglasses, closely-cropped sideburns, tattoos
on their arms and carried walkmans. And so he com-
pleted his description the driver. – They seemed wap-
ero (so they call the middle class snobby) who
sometimes hop on for short distances.

Curiosity led me to seek more details and despite the
revolutionary practice of hidden information, I had
access to the records of the expedient of the protagonist who police call Tamakun, a radio character forty

years ago, who described himself as Wandering Avenger, because they say, that when this young dude attacks, he shouts he's coming to get even, that he'll never be caught. Certainly very nimble, he moves quickly for assaulting and escaping.

His resume reveals no known father, a mother waitress by trade, synonymous of B-girl or prostitute, who abandons him when he was three years old and leaves him under the care of the alcoholic grandmother who abuses him and dies twenty months later. During the next twelve years he wanders from neighbors, group-home, juvenile centers, supervised probation, care centers and rehabilitation schools and even family placement on trial. Finally there is an annex of a psychosocial study and comments of the Minors' Attorney from the Public Prosecutor's Office that state a maniacal obsession for injuring any adult woman that he bumps into.

Tiger Face as he is nicknamed because his body is striped with scars, he is the typical case of a repeat offender, he comes from San Pablito of Mamera slum, and I went up there to learn about his environment, the hill from there to here, a landscape that is not exactly bucolic . Cold bloodedly and patiently I went to talk with other teens and children who have the same aspect of those glue sniffers and anise consumers I posed as a new nurse from the nearby health clinic and I was to meet the neediest people of that service.

With fearful responses of intermittent phrases, due to distrust and fear because of the fierce raid last night, I could assemble half part of the profile, a puzzle – They tell me he gets into quarrels – He doesn't duff up garlic with candy but with macho and brother – He is a top dude, he distributes grands that he snatches out there – and tells blowies a lot, he says that his mother is a kick-ass and a TV actress. But somewhere else – He jumps on light concrete slabs when there is a donnybrook. He knows how to hole up so the fuzz don't throw him in the hoosegow – By sheer luck, but always manages to run away from the pigs – We haven't seen him here in a coon's age – Maybe they liquidated him – The crook has its legend…

They are just some of the most understandable phrases by the context. But how much longer can this jargon be understood without a pocket dictionary?

It seemed to me being in a huge village, expansive, densely populated and undermined by rancor. Observing my city from that point of view, I felt it as a camp, and a concentration one, increasingly narrow and on the side, I accepted that ultimately I was the marginal, eyes covered, that after so much dealing with the news I ended up believing that it's just a story, that maybe it was time to catch if that borderline is a mirage, barrier, pit or goal of this so-called revolution by the debuting president commander.

When will my lucky day come, I know it will be before I die, surely, my luck will change... Waiting for
my luck I was, but my life another direction took, sur-
viving a reality, of which I could not escape... When
will my lucky day come...

ALL OF US IN A WEEK

1

THIS MINI-BUS IS LEAVING friends. Stop listening to old stories, hear mine. Listen, today Wednesday, a terrible day for traffic, at the center in the middle of the center and by travelers with a message, I bring you a story of the naughtiness of a girl very tired of the homework and family errands. Dawn breaks   beautifully that day and she decides it is only for playing, playing and more playing. Then she calls her grandmother, between retirement and laziness, giving her the mother's lunch bag who was an employee of a public office on the outskirts of said village, and with a quality performance asks her to substitute her – Once, grandmother, at least once in your life because today I need to play, play and nothing but play.

It is understood; in this case the plea is an order.

It was the rainy season and the hurricane winds roared. The cautious granddaughter covered the messenger with her read rain coat, hooded and with a cape, no hats – Go on, go now, but take the long way, in a bus or a jeepney, because the subway is short and clean but more expensive and somebody can rob you or push you.

Everything was possible in this village of terror.

The biddy rambler goes out well groomed and from afar she sees a plain, mannish man, hairy, big teeth who also waits for a tin can on wheels, of this same ilk. Closely inhaling his smell and scanning his body hair she thinks how much she wishes to go for a walk to the green hill tightly holding this strong fellow's arm that helps her to climb the rungs of a small bus identical to this one. It would be great that the trip would be endless to ride together to the station.

– Where are you trying to get? – Who, me? Getting older and you? – Maybe I won't even get anywhere near that – Wow, you're so tall – To hold you better.

Thus begins the adventure of once upon a time.

The friend is not the big bad wolf but smoothness of macho sheep, warm and gentle. And of so much excitement the protagonist forgets how continues the narrative and total line, her starving daughter is left without lunch.

Hours pass and her family realizes that something terrible might have happened, because in the afternoons, after four o'clock, the missing fulfills her home rituals. They request the search and rescue services from a crowd of hunters who go from pillar to post, park, hospital, cemetery, morgue, supermarket, mass transportation stations, where not? Until they finally find the very lost frolicking at the home of her knight, a cinder blocks hovel at the west of the populated village. Eaten away by termites, and over the door, a tempting plate invites you with an "Everything is done here".

Yes, I am the Red-colored Cap, she told the searchers. Don't shoot, don't split open his belly, don't take him away, I have finally been able to make the revolution, it has been the romp of love which no rhythmic gymnastics or measures competition, or strict duty of weekly schedule, or smiling couple in a social review. I'm even capable of swallowing a full mandrake root to conceive again, because only with him, loving is to bet without rivals, a challenge without cheating, real racket.

And I can't tell what you are expecting, the details of the ultimate play, because there was so much craving, that with kisses and nibbles the voluptuous was devouring her partner with zeal, born musician, lumberjack by force and handyman by despair.

But it continues with another story. By uniting with the man-ram, she almost always sullen and swaying in the swings on the edge of nerves, she became affectionate and darling... *You make me feel so young, as the spring that has sprung. Every time I see you grin, I am s happy...* Her usual hump inclination gave way to a bearing of a svelte lass, that cement hut unfinished outside was comfortable inside and turned into a castle, the dirty adjacent pond was a limpid lagoon. *When you speak, I want to play hide and seek, I want to bounce with the moon as it were a toy balloon...* And together they realized the moral of The Three Little Pigs, you know. Which of the three cabins could survive the excesses of nature and wild animals? Puf's was built with rustic tiles. Pif's and Paf's are built, one with shiny straw sticks, the other with gleaming planks, both with pretty facades plummet at the slightest breeze.

In that squalid shack, designed with cheap and rude materials, she wouldn't dwell eternity, but for good part of good life without the stalking of evil goblins. Music and love are journeys with time at a standstill that nullifies distances. Without reproach, it would be simple the act of leaving perceiving they could not sustain each other, when they would see falling one of the columns that erected that transparent and generous trust. Because love skips some unfaithful act, soft is the shell. What it doesn't admit is disloyalty, duplicity matter of soul. And there is much bleeding at childbirth, at any age when you from traditional to provisional... *You and I are like a couple of kids cross country running...* It is sad that the end was about to happen in a landslide due to heavy rain. It was not so. They still form a beam, rescued by the only standing pillar when the rest turns into ruins. Hand giving hand... *You make me feel that there are songs to sing, bells to toll, arrows to throw...*

Everything comes to an end, and so does our fable of today. The great kingdom of this world, so called the chroniclers the time for playing, playing and playing that lasted this story, and if you can think of something else, you know, you count on me... *And though I am an old gray-haired woman, I'll keep on feeling this way, because with you I'm young.*

We reached our destination. To the bus stop. Until next time...

2

THERE ARE TALES I DON'T LIKE TO TELL, not
even on a sweet Thursday as today, prelude of little
Saturday, because they are parts of the most shameful
criminal record. Look how difficult to believe that father and mother throw their children as waste into the
dangerous neighboring forest, on the pretext that they
cannot feed them. As so, as one counts starts, face up
on a meadow of fine grass in an open summer night,
they are saying that the innocent children seek the
path of return stumbling on a little marzipan house
smelling of ginger, that a lovely old lady shelters them
with a delicious dinner and cages them asleep because
she is a professional child eater.

As the nasty parents of Hansel and Gretel, the killer
doesn't satiate her greedy hunting preys in that same
forest, or collects fruits, or fishes in the rivers. To
make matters worse, she was already filthy rich and
her evil ways allowed her to have fancy pastry to en-
snare her victims. Believe it. There are freeloaders of
innocent poverty.

Don't ask because if I answer you'll know how this
telling that I don't want to tell is perfected with the
military. In our forest of third or even fifth world, no

excuses, every day around the world, fifty little children starve. And the story continues.

Instinctively, the siblings imprisoned in that little jail for bait and extermination, eat very little knowing that if they fatten, in the blink of an eye they will be the cannibal's delicacy. Thus, they prolong their hunger to earn a chance on life, no matter how minimal. Living is the first commandment.

One day, when she rose earlier, the sorceress puts on makeup as for a feast and begins to prepare seasoning for the roast. She asks the girl for help because she needs more fuel for the sacrifice pit which emits poisonous smoke in such a quantity that erases the vision of the environment. As they say, digging your own grave. And Gretel not beating around the bushes, pushes her into the fire and frees Hansel.

The amazing thing is when the storyteller returns the pipsqueaks to give Mom and Dad the treasures of the murderer who is already dust. Such a huge reward for scoundrels. What nerve, a crime without punishment. More difficult it is to fall for the story that children as keen as them to avoid the killing do not notice the monstrous truth. Maybe they did not want or assume such great desolation. The thing is that safe presence parents build you a prefab home, internal, well stocked where you safely dwell against the inclemency. Careful, exaggerating the need fatally leads to all indifference be the living death of the blues. In addition, an abandoned, plus another, plus another, are people who will seek in a tyrant wearing an olive green uniform or red shirt, a father, that lost or unknown warranty. Story without happy ending, see?

And it's logical, used to say my father while he dragged me to the musical events in theaters, squares and to the Coney Island of the East to record my songs in a forty-five vinyl, don't laugh, please, I sang very nicely – Music is our natal chart. Note that from the heartbeat of your mother, with heat and darkness, you are initiated in the cadence of rhythm. Then they throw you to the cold light that binds you. It turns out that before seeing and touching, smelling and tasting; you are a melody crying in whimper for your entrance into the harsh and beautiful world.

You finally realize, don't you? Since what the bolero singers accurately call it the organ of feeling, we carry in our blood the percussion of being and the melodic cry of being born. A place for its commonness is forgotten. I say it, among many, the very wise and despicable Mr. Perogrullo. Astonishing is sometimes the obvious, isn't it?

3

I TAKE ADVANTAGE of this long line at the gas station to retell you the tale, I will narrate it as it actually happened, who knows. It turns out that the parents were not barbarians, no. They, on the contrary, were confident without reservations on the talent of their children and their strategic plan was to take the high risk of sending their offspring to get rid of the voracious maniacal that was decimating the child population of the area with her horrific practice. Yes, that was what happened. I think. And when I told you in detail about the real fact, I complete it with another similar one but never the same ... My mom then told me, since I wore shorts, that I would be attracted by a double-sided figure, and when he seduction would finish, she would leave me nostalgic, so I would sing the blues at night ... it is that story in which also suffered for this detestable habit, those seven brothers, perhaps in the same forest but were luckier, since the smallest, Thumbelina, has the chagrin of hearing the macabre plan, she outlines with pebbles the path through which his father leads them and return to the site that was not exactly a home, shocking, isn't it?

The next day the ruthless repeat their abominable betrayal, but this time the girl outlines the way with breadcrumbs and the birds of that nefarious necropolis, that is, the forest, eat them. The hostess is also changed. This is a friendly housewife and the ogre is her husband who also suffers from an appetite for the fresh meat of children, and getting to work, before the usual time, orders his wife to prepare them for breakfast, as seven normal fried eggs. This is what a wise woman of our time called banality of evil. The revolution eats its children, says history, remember that.

In this case the previous confinement was none other than the bedroom of the seven favorite girls of the gargantuan, crowned in gold even to sleep. So learn, brain is better than brawn, and Thumbelina, who cannot sleep from worry, but who doesn't live by her wits, comes up with the rescuing barter... *The evening breeze sounds and makes the trees cry, the moon hides its light when you get the blues at night, and believe me, that nightingale will sing the saddest song because he knows that this is wrong and he is so right* ... The little girl loves life with all her dear ones, then she passes the gold diadems on to her head and of her brothers, so at dawn the wicked beheaded his own infantas. It's horrible that the innocent suffer for the craziness of a mad glutton but what is good for the goose is good for the gander, survival is law and to comply with daily.

And the feats are extended in this underworld manual which are these tales, because the ruffian seeks revenge from seven-league boots. In his espionage flight he cannot reach the youngsters and falls exhausted at the foot of a tree, for sure in the same graveyard, I meant forest. Thumbelina and company take the quick boots, sell the crowns, buy mills, wheat grains, a lot of land for sowing and become farmers. But the story is another because they don't even think on going back to the house where they were born; they distrust those adults who shed the blood of their young brash, without shame or embarrassment. Think and think, can you imagine a kingdom of villains founded only to procreate and eliminate idle people? But it happens here. It has supernatural nuances and it seems a tale, doesn't it?

When I decide and retell your about Thumbelina, you will see how the tiny tot managed during the drought crisis and frequent seven lean years. She became the fastest cards deliverer of the universe, of course using the glutton's fast boots, who died of cholera or dengue. Allegedly, although the inventor of the famous story never signed, to the best of our knowledge, this double final happy end ... *I went to large cities, I heard great speeches, but I just know something, my mother was right, there are blues in the night...*

I spend the long day doing that, telling stories, I try not to scream or growl or howl, not jump or lunge or walk on all fours, not gnaw or tear or swallow. When the sun sink, a dry weeping overflows me and with lunatic thirst I invoke a jazz, ballad, moaning of the solitaire in divine blue and profane, sign of redemption ... The night breeze shakes the trees tenderly ... *you open your arms and enclose me, tenderly ...*

4

SATURDAY EVE, listen then. I don't come on Saturdays. Remember, it was always an ugly duckling the famous one. When her mother gave birth for the first time, there were six embryos, five evenly matched and one very different. The friends, noticing that very rare specimen, they comforted the parents with great intention – Don't worry, it is clear that due to a slight genetic error, it is a little guan and not a duck.

Five beautiful creatures burst the shell on time; the sixth and different one took a little longer. Even then, it required more heat to grow.

She finally broke the membrane, a day like this one, facing the sun, unique and fragile, sophisticated and difficult. And from the nest she began to feel the distinctive mark. – You sure are strange – Nobody even takes you to the entryway – Stop believing in the lies of Hans Christian Andersen and the Grimm Brothers and read a dictionary, of those books for the stories I tell you – Are you going to keep singing and swaying without stopping? – With your obsession for Frank Sinatra you scratched all his records ... *My friend, I say it clearly, and I state my case of which I am certain. I have lived a full life, I went through each of the ways but more, much more than that, I did it my way...*

Easily approving school subjects didn't bring her friends. During recess she was left aside, because she belonged to another class, they said that she was very uncouth and simpleton.

One day she told her mother – I'm not going back to that henhouse because they spit in their own well without realizing they might to drink from it. I'm going to another corral.

And so she left for the opposite area where each student had a reputation for being disgusting, thick and no last name. Also there she was isolated in the playground – She behaves as the rich ones – She is not one of us – She seems from another place – She doesn't pray or communicate, she doesn't make the sign of the holy cross or confesses – Lank hair-very fair-skinned – A midget and scrawny. She is very full of herself.

When she received the elementary school certificate, she went to visit that first school and nobody recognized her. Upon discovering who she was, the old schoolmates surrounded her, nodding just for a while. In the span of a sneeze they cast her again into the corner. This time she felt anger, hatred, desire for revenge because they went away among derisive laughs and murmurs. Then she promised herself that some day she would fly over the swing to boast about her elevation... *Sometimes I regretted it, but I did what I had to do, I thought it was right, and much more than that, I did it my way...*

She was a more than a rare bird. Neither an ugly duckling, nor a cute swan and much less a heron. In any flock they felt her as from another, and she had to admit herself as peculiar ... *I loved, I laughed, I cried, I lost, I won, now with tears, it seems so moving. To think I did all that, I can say not cautiously, oh no, it would not be me. Yes I did, in my way* ... Beautiful melody, sing with me then.

Perhaps her formidable blue or greenish prince, some other model of rare plumage, of identical or similar species, lurching through the same difficult route and at the unpredictable encounter forge the disparate solitudes. Only then I would tell them that perhaps they lived happily ever after in a land so unreal that it was never a nation, and allows them to be one and strangers, in pairs or lonely.

There are those who are bullshit, and if you believe in that two of a kind, you make life a tormentor or risible or delightful fantastic tale, depends. *After all, what is a person, what has she got. If it's not for herself, she wrecks. Then she must say what she truly feels, and to the words of one who kneels. The record shows I took the blows, my way.* Blessed Sinatra.

My selected Friday for the special rejuvenating day by day. The Voice and Satchmo, and Caruso and More and Oscar D'Leon. From the first syllable, each one identical only to himself. Listen and then, for sure, there arises from each one, its sacred list. Don't let them to steal from you what they are with the revolutionary stories.

5

SINCE ON SUNDAYS THERE are fewer crowds in these clunkers, the environment causes me to sharpen the incredible tangle of that miller who divides his inheritance. For the younger and weaker, only and incredibly, he leaves a cat. For you to sweat buckets to make a living with neatness and effort, the oldest receives his mill and the middle son his donkey.

But this rogue cat can talk, gets to the point and asks his new boss for the implements that restore the honor to the most rascal. Polished boots, hat, tail coat and gabardine trousers, flirtatious catlike stamp of the one that from the fifth world is initiated in politics, as now, in disguise.

As customary, one first courts the powerful on duty. Rabbit stolen in hand with fine glove, our indomitable bandit prostrates – Your Lordship, this is a gift from my master, the Marquis of Carabas.

That gesture of intrigue multiplies the time required for the sovereign to personally know the generous subject who is represented by an intermediary.

The wily manager keeps track of the highest authority and discovers that he's ridding in his brand new unmarked car, at a very high speed through the congested city, en route to the periphery of the district, at fixed times.

The more conducive afternoon is, when with his binoculars he envisions the commotion of the entourage instructing his obedient owner – You shed your clothes, you scream you have been robbed at gunpoint by the thugs, you keep quiet, I'll take care of the rest.

The art of cajoling. The ruler, convinced that his endearing admirer has been the victim of the frenzied criminals, shakes his hand and dictates his lackeys urgent compensation measures – Take one of my suits from the luggage so that my beloved friend may greet my only daughter here present, because in these conditions a first encounter is not suitable.

Of course, she quickly falls in love precisely because she has time to evaluate the attributes of the future husband scanning him from afar almost naked. And he swears he will love her until death do them part because his counselor reminds him that a rich bride is never ugly.

Meanwhile the next emporium manager gets ahead of the retinue, he greases the palms of the underpaid slaves who working their fingers to the bone asphalt the route through which passes the very royal government of that domain, ordering to repeat by heart –

The Marquis of Carabas is the sole owner of these lands, fields and basins.

Of course to achieve its goal The Cat in Boots takes other provisions. In addition to the already mentioned tips, he harangues with a smooth tongue the ignorant who by piecework are pulling weed with a hoe, he swears and assures that he will fulfill the promise of enabling the invasion of that feud once they eliminate the current owner, a bloody landowner from the old regime who illegally appropriated these wastelands that belong to the people. What happens, he proclaims, with the revolutionary process about to happen. A cliché for the one that discards.

A thousand years of forgiveness, for a thief capable of stealing from a thief and with heroic labia?

The third maneuver is even more edifying. Our bold feline as goes in as if he owned the place in the house of the same aristocrat stripped of his land, a real animal that accepts the challenge without suspecting in the least that there is something fishy going on – Mr. Magician, evil tongues say that you have the ability to become other beings alive and ticking. Frankly, my Master and I do not believe that you can't even become a miserable rodent.

It should be pointed out that the honorable Prime Minister did not need to drag or scratch or wag his tail and not even meow during his exercise of power behind and above the throne. His wisdom in this position was exemplary and legendary. Fraud, theft, incitement to commit a crime, violation of privacy, willfully and with malice thought homicide, complete farce of law, constitute the Magna Charta of that remarkable kingdom, whose memory is preserved for posterity and which legacy can you register in our daily work for where there is a civic muddle there arises the drill, a picturesque laughing puss that does not always wear booties or buckled shoes he can also wear espadrilles and poor garments, but he applies a similar method with high, medium and even low profile. Beware of those clowns.

…The one who only lives to make money, lives and existence that is not necessarily solid. As the one who works for fame, there is no guarantee that he elevates his name. The only effort that really brings joy is the type of men and women do, if you fall in love…

Snip, snap snout, this tale's not told out, for now. Pardon me if a use fancy words. I want you to be educated and learn to speak nicely and correctly. It so happens that a fourth chapter is missing, almost clandestine because there are many storytellers that tell it. What happens is that time is almost up for the villain, judge and executioner with fangs and tiger claws of a tiger that was defeated by a lion, and so on thereafter until the final beast succumbed to a virus of the jungle. The inner workings are long and a never ending story. Meanwhile not even doubt it, it's a lie that justice must be a marble statue and a slender babe wearing a tunic, carrying a balance and blindfolded. Neither Eros nor Cupid, gods of love shoot only young men. No way. At least it is thought bursts the first bloom in the old girl, delirious girl old, torn jeans, canvas shoes, her thin matted hair tied in a ponytail. Prostitute or pure, or deranged, that will tell it the eye of the beholder. When they decide it, the naive and the intellectual and the perverse, a stuffed animal can be a corny gizmo, a weapon of war or a pet. For sure, the least like Venus walks very slowly, but jumps the Hopscotch on one foot, and always green, she safely arrives. And is that the unusual happens, everything has to come, let us sing ... You will not regret if you get it. It is the best job of all. At midnight, shaking hands peering at the starry sky, knowing that there is someone waiting for you in the doorpost. If you try to get that job, you will. And if you get it, tell me how you did it... Otherwise, you must know, there are stories that will never be tales. They are truths in the soul.

6

ON IDLENESS MONDAY and of lunatics note that it is a pack of lies that a wicked queen consulted her magic mirror on who was Miss Universe of her time, and after hearing the response she decided to erase from the face of the earth the chosen one, her step-daughter Snow White. No. That was a matter of inheritance as the most beautiful was the only daughter of noble ancestry. And jealousy by greed damage with rage the most angelical brain and lead it to madness. That's the story.

There is also tall tale that the ranger saved the candidate out of mercy. He sensed that sooner or later he would be discovered, and the downcast king would drag him by the hair to the gallows. No. The thing is that the renowned forest of red varmints already extended its fateful fame throughout the new empire.

Much less should you believe that Snow White was well regarded in her home servitude by the seven dwarfs, who were so not because of their physical size of eunuchs, but by their very low moral stature. Where there is too much something is missing and their social status matched their stinginess, both were news across the borders.

Working uncomfortable and for free in the house of seven bosses in exchange for a small dwelling was intolerable, much more when the days and months go by , and the girl has no boyfriend and drowns in tears every evening on the kitchen counter, in an alien place, with no hope for change.

Hence, when the stepmother reappears disguised as a fruiterer beggar and offers her a poisoned apple, Snow White eats it with relish because her bosses had rationed the food.

The relative had heard of her resurrection by gossip that was no grandmother's tales. She knew then that the pocket and mind pygmy had violated their own rule of meanness employing a beautiful woman, very white and enigmatic origin. Then the opponent reacted to remove her, this time personally.

The heartless dwarves wept itself despite the supposed death of their cheap handmaiden. It hurt them to lose a sleep-in housekeeper and at no cost. Moreover, their greed went so far that they postponed the burial to peacefully go on Sunday, their day off, to remove from the funeral forest the rotten timbers they'd use as a casket.

But they ignored the end of the fable. In that interval a young gold digger appeared, so licentious that he almost immediately fornicates with whom, by famished, seemed a corpse. Only that the girl, languishing

155

from overwork and chronic malnutrition, regains consciousness. Nothing to do with exorcism and incantations. At that age and at mine, the male taste of a kiss penetrates with unusual power into virginal entrails or melts the floe of the most shabby and sleepy. Ha ha.

The insatiable and the resuscitated known each other already well awake and manage to escape the castrated one. Perhaps, before getting pregnant and out of shape, Snow White could win the international beauty contest and toured the world as a successful developer of whitening cosmetics and she was almost the death the one already divorced from her father and who continued in full misery and envy, breaking mirrors because she seeks and seeks the one that will return her million-dollar image.

Something similar happens with Cinderella because mother-in-law and stepsisters relegate her to the burner to prevent her from exercising the aristocratic privileges that come from being the first-born by paternal line. They also subject her to extreme labor without remuneration in sight. They don't even give her a dress to change when she gets covered with soot.

She has to be a fairy because she is winged but with a magic wand and everything, matchmaker by trade who figuring out the ancestry of that domestic worker, finds the important reason to fix that mess with a glass slipper, a float and other midnight tales. The words you don't understand are in the dictionary. Look for them because if you don't know how to speak you won't find a good job.

It is easy to assume the void and previous gray scenario prior to marriage, where the nymphs, in a mood of blues, were singing All by myself ... *All by myself in the morning, entirely by myself at night, sitting unhappy here, playing solitaire, watching the watch. I would like to lay my troubles on someone's shoulder. I hate getting older, all alone...*

Although at the beginning it came to links for convenience, you should know that a true love is no tale and culminates in close friendship. When the rest is damaged, there grazes the reliable holding hands ... *If we can be the best of lovers, while being the best of friends, if we try to do better every day, then, with a little luck, the music never ends ...*

You might say, I think, why the efforts of this chatty in turning the nut and telling gobbledygook of fibs. Oh, oh, my friends, I'm finally trying to be somewhat realistic, falsifying the known deceit to assume some truth and meanwhile the whole world rejoices and we are entertained, how about them apples?

7

TODAY, STUBBORNS' AND FIGHTERS' TUESDAY, it pleases me remembering the itinerant who stops in Hamelin. He's very fatigued, hungry and thirsty. Nobody looks at the one arriving with a backpack and sandals because all the people gather in the square, raising hands against the mayor for his inability to solve the essential problem, which could it, be? Yes, you guessed it. Public larceny that has left the settlers without sustenance or reserves. All the provisions in currency and species went into the pockets of those obese rats whose positions have a high-sounding title, namely, prosecutor, president of the court of law, finance minister, head of the parliament, chairman of the investigative commission, and stop counting.

How to end once and for all with the scourge of phonies, the desperate population of Hamelin wonders that has already tried their extermination by routine methods to activate the mouse holes but without obtaining cure or improvement. Angry cries against the portal of the bigwig indicate that patience was filled while the humble stranger is silent pining for lodging. But suddenly he stands in front of the neighbors, draws his instrument, gestures to foster silence and without boasting calms tempers with these words. – I promise the get the rats from their burrows, leaving unmasked their crime in broad daylight and free this place of these crooks. In return I ask that you host me right away for a few hours, and properly pay for my service. I just know some music and from that I barely subsist. Then, they make a verbal agreement, much more reliable than a paper signed by the notary. Our hero puts his lips on the luminous trumpet and makes vibrate the light houses in the village. And what happened. An event. There are shattered only those with glass roof. In addition, the shiver that causes the avalanche of chords with white, black, eighth notes and thirty-second notes sung with personal accent, seeps every corner, rekindles the fire of chimneys and sets on fire the tails of all that "ratcracy". Upon hearing the melodic Open Sesame, its members, Ali Baba and the forty thieves, and without resistance, they come out of the caves and enchanted follow the footprint of the melodious echo. It was magic that brought together the ideal with the staff in this action, this is no tale. Nonperforming evil creeps in a row to the cells where a real court sentences for the happy destiny of that region... *How do to make this music to continue playing, how do you manage it to stay, how do you prevent the very fast decay of the song* ... And there was a decree of regional joy and comedy contests and festivities and hallelujah choruses and the gatekeeper was given the keys of the city to always be their guest and leader. And you know, the good name is more

159

important than a gemstone. Cheers! Come sing with me ... *This could happen only to a guy like me, and can only happen in a town like this. My kind of town is this, yes, that smiles at you, and every time I wander around, you call me back home ... A town that never, never lets you down. It's my kind of jazzmatazz, and has all that jazz. It is a town that never, ever disappoints you...*

MY WONDERFUL COUNTRY

1

I AM TELLING A STORY with this ones that is god for any day, and since I'm unemployed again, pursued by an alleged crime that I don't know I seek refuge and I tell you that recently with no job or hope of finding one, well into the afternoon, I was resting at the edge of a waterfall in the park of streams when I heard some very quick steps.

They were of a famous white rabbit, so elegant that he wears gloves, an umbrella and a watch.

For a boring afternoon it was good the surprise of that intruder because in general that recluse animal is shy, constantly changing lair, runs more quickly if you observe him, cantankerous to get caught and hard to subdue.

I'll be late, he repeated. And seeing him go into the hole open in the trunk of the chestnut tree, by boredom, I decided to follow him.

Entering at will in the night is inevitable, as the little death by passion. I fell into the vertigo of a swinging in continuous abyss... *Dancing in the dark till the tune ends, we danced in the dark and this ends very soon, we waltzed in the wonder of why we are her. Time is short. We are here, let's go...*

I squinted because of the intense glow of a huge and empty hall, with multiple closed doors, and which only way out seemed to be a narrow corridor, also blocking locked up, and let me tell you, there disappeared the furtive rabbit. I can share my shiver if I make a confidence. Since always, I flee from the panic a cloister causes in me. Break you wings and unleash the hidden dragon that you tie with good manners in respect and dread of the denial.

Gradually curios objects arise. A small three-legged table, a little golden key and a piece of cake with his label Eat me. The key didn't fit into any lock. With no other choice or witnesses because I fully. enjoyed the forbidden fruit. Savoring such divine sweet revived me into a beautiful, young, strong, seductive and powerful person. I forgot the prison. Now, everything seemed possible. If believed in it, I would say it was revolution.

It is difficult and shameful but you have to admit Mr. Perogrullo its simplicity that nothing and no one comes, and remains and doesn't depart forever. Believe me, happiness is a printed word in the index and who registers it with interest, dos find, happy hours. The line of notes appears on every score but there is only rhythm and melody when it's given to you outside, inside.... *Waiting for the light of a new love to light the night, I possess you love, and we can reach together, music dancing in the dark* ... So much sudden greatness made me losing her own and others' measure. I could not get through an ordinary space. Squatting I could barely glimpse from a lower slit, the delight of a wonderful garden how to reach its pleasures? Oh, everything green needs a swing.

With such height and posture I was stiff with cramps. I sit on the ground to mourn, mourn and mourn and then on that table appears a blue bottle with a label praying Drink Me. How to reject the viscous liquid which being seminal irrigates you shrinks and wrinkles you submissive? You are so diminished that the puddle of your own tears becomes a river and you are swept along, tiny, about to be consumed and disappear.

Perhaps you haven't realized it. Cooking is alchemy of household witches. On the one hand, if you prepare jam, as confectioner your success lies in duly keeping to the dosages indicated in the recipe gird. It gets spoiled if you measure at your whim. On the other hand, it is the freest laboratory to imagine combinations that take you to enjoy love and friendship, a moment of lips and tongues quivering in conspiratorial pleasure.

I practice it often but that day I scolded myself strongly than ever. You expand, you become a giant, and you lose control of your feet that go where you haven't wanted. And if you diminish too much, you become weak and sad. Exact moment when reappears the little rabbit with its litany. *It's getting late, It's getting late for me...*

My problem at that time was nothing at all understanding who I am, because I've always known I'm no Tom, Dick and Harry let alone a chip of cheating revolutions... Neither if I could flee because I was motionless cornered. My dilemma was to grow or not, for what, for whom and how far. In this meditation I'm regaining my normal size and I burst into laughter by the immense joy of beating awake after my maddening nightmare. Because in a short time I went through so many changes that I am never being what I was or will be. I was new but I regained my being. The caterpillar is very calm because he knows that smoothly he is going to turn into a chrysalis and butterfly. But the sudden turns without control or fixed center ordered to you by a king for example, lead to helplessness and produce bad temper. You have already noticed it in my tale and song. Then I have to invent because I never remember in the same way. I think that while I was laughing when appeared Eugenio de Andrade and said, listen carefully ... *I know I 'm alive and on Earth I'm growing up, and not because I'm more powerful, or wiser, or more wealthy. As the supplicant mouth of another mouth, as a brief white and silent flame, as the wind in the darkness in the twilight that opens, I feel I'm alive; I live growing up your torso, at your side...*

Now is necessary to cut a bit this very long story that explores wonders and I can list a few. I survive in a ditch full of pink snails listening fascinated the tales of a leathery red oyster, a red and black raven laughing for no apparent reason in the middle of the yelling, a team of crabs whisper about my stubborn resistance, the bar of summoned parakeets guffawing applauding the identical babble of the commanding big ugly bird, in changing clothes for each appearance but always red-green, a fleshy fungus with half one can enlarge and with the other decrease, and of which, just in case, I preserve pieces in the pocket of my apron, nasty animals competing without game rules, servants of the salary the king gives them, or queen, all faces look like cold fish because they are threatened and are scared. There is a ball game with the tyranny that resolves with the big talk and concludes decreeing haphazardly cutting heads under the enigmatic smile of an invisible cat, but we know, he orders from the island of happiness from where everyone wants and we want to flee. And a knowledgeable hatter, alas, who says that we are all raving lunatics killing the free life in that frenetic official scramble.

Then calls me the other Eugenio, Montejo, and we traveled trough... My vertical century and full of theories... I cross Marx Street, Freud Street... I walk

166

around a bank of this century with its wars, its post-wars and its Hitler drum far away between blood and abysses...

And the silver headed hatter, with his vast experience, again recommends capturing time, because it's a very fast and sketchy hare. He adds that for an illiterate old age is winter but harvest time for the wise... And in the middle of that insanity Fred Astaire raises me and I'm Ginger Rogers because... *Though love is old, what if the song is old, through we both can be young... Dancing in the night...* And I listen to them because I know my story and I fully comply with it, especially now, at the conclusion of the trial, mock battle of cards since accuser, referee and jury are the same person, a new king, a very real process which verdict condemns me to suspend this dream. I'm guilty for insisting on absurd fantasies as this one of visiting a country so far without wonders, where gray hair remains raw and the flavorful fruit doesn't fall ripe.

I'll seek lawyers who defend my right to reinvent, believe and return to my country of wonders, telling hundred times whatever pleases me illuminated by this bible called glow that came to the manuscript of an unsurpassed storyteller centuries ago. Fearing that his rebelliousness against the cruel reign they called victorious would burn him in a modern bonfire of real inquisition, he disguised people as characters, he dedicated to me in the title, loving and gentle, during a very long walk along the water of all times.

Table of Contents